Claiming King's Baby

MAUREEN CHILD

First published in Great Britain 2010
Large Print edition 2010
Harlequin Mills & Boon Limited,
Eton House, 18-24 Paradise Road,
Richmond, Surrey TW9 1SR

LP

© Maureen Child 2009

ISBN: 978 0 263 21619 6

Harlequin Mills & Boon policy is to use papers that
are natural, renewable and recyclable products and
made from wood grown in sustainable forests. The
logging and manufacturing process conform to the legal
environmental regulations of the country of origin.

Printed and bound in Great Britain
by CPI Antony Rowe, Chippenham, Wiltshire

MAUREEN CHILD

is a California native who loves to travel. Every chance they get, she and her husband are taking off on another research trip. An author of more than sixty books, Maureen loves a happy ending and still swears that she has the best job in the world. She lives in Southern California with her husband, two children and a gold retriever with delusions of grandeur.

You can contact Maureen via her website www.maureenchild.com

To the Estrada Family:
Steve, Rose, Alicia,
Letti, Patti and Amanda.
Good friends. Great neighbours.

We love you guys.

<u>One</u>

Justice King opened the front door and faced his past.

She stood there staring at him out of pale blue eyes he'd tried desperately to forget. Her long, light red hair whipped around her head in a cold, fierce wind, and her delectable mouth curved into a cynical half smile.

"Hello, Justice," said a voice that haunted his dreams. "Been a while."

Eight months and twenty-five days, he thought but didn't say. His gaze moved over her in a quick but thorough inspection. She was tall, with the same stubborn tilt to her chin that he remembered and the same pale sprinkle of freckles across her nose. Her full breasts rose and fell quickly with each of her rapid breaths, and that more than anything else told him she was nervous.

Well, then, she shouldn't have come.

His gaze locked back on hers. "What're you doing here, Maggie?"

"Aren't you going to invite me in?"

"Nope," he said flatly. One thing he didn't need was to have her close enough to touch again.

"Is that any way to talk to your wife?" she asked and walked past him into the ranch house.

His wife.

Automatically, his left thumb moved to play with the gold wedding band he'd stopped wearing the day he had allowed her to walk away. Memories crashed into his mind, and he closed his eyes against the onslaught.

But nothing could stop the images crowding his brain. Maggie, naked, stretched out on his bed, welcoming him. Maggie, shouting at him through her tears. Maggie, leaving without a backward glance. And last, Justice saw himself, closing the door behind her and just as firmly shuttering away his heart.

Nothing had changed.

They were still the same people they'd been when they married and when they split.

So he pulled himself together, and closed the front door behind them. Then he turned to face her.

Watery winter sunlight poured from the skylight onto the gleaming wood floors and glanced off the mirror hanging on the closest wall. A pedestal table held an empty cobalt vase—there'd been no flowers in this hall since Maggie left—and the silence in the house slammed down on top of them both.

Seconds ticked past, marked only by the tapping of Maggie's shoe against the floor.

Justice waited her out, knowing that she wouldn't be able to be quiet for long. She never had been comfortable with silence. Maggie was the most talkative woman he'd ever known. Damned if he hadn't missed that.

Three feet of empty space separated them and still, Justice felt the pull of her. His body was heavy and aching and everything in him clawed at him to reach out for her. To ease the pain of doing without her for far too long.

Yet he called on his own reserves of strength to keep from taking what he'd missed so badly.

"Where's Mrs. Carey?" Maggie asked suddenly, her voice shattering the quiet.

"She's on vacation." Justice cursed inwardly, wishing to hell his housekeeper had picked some other time to take a cruise to Jamaica.

"Good for her," Maggie said, then tipped her head to one side. "Glad to see me?"

Glad wasn't the word he'd use. *Stunned*

would be about right. When Maggie had left, she'd sworn that he would never see her again. And he hadn't, not counting the nights she appeared in his dreams just to torment him.

"What are you doing here, Maggie?"

"Well, now, that's the question, isn't it?"

She turned away and walked slowly down the hall, bypassing the more formal living room before stepping into the great room. Justice followed, watching as she looked around the room as if reacquainting herself with the place.

She looked from the floor-to-ceiling bookshelves on two walls to the river stone hearth, tall and wide enough for a man to stand in it upright. The log walls, with the white chinking between them that looked like horizontal striping. The plush chairs and sofas she'd bought for the room, gathered together into conversation areas, and the wide bank of windows that displayed an unimpeded view of the ranch's expansive front yard. Ancient trees spread shade across most of the lawn, flowers in the neatly tended beds dipped and swayed with the ocean wind and from a distance came the muffled roar of the ranch tractor moving across the feed grain fields.

"You haven't changed anything," she whispered.

"Haven't had time," he lied.

"Of course." Maggie spun around to face him and her eyes were flashing.

Justice felt a surge of desire shoot through him with the force of a lightning strike. Her temper had always had that effect on him. They'd been like oil and water, sliding against each other but never really blending into a cohesive whole. And maybe that was part of the attraction, he mused.

Maggie wasn't the kind of woman to change for a man. She was who she was, take her or leave her. He'd always wanted to take her. And God help him, if she came too close to him right now, he'd take her again.

"Look," she said, those blue eyes of hers still snapping with sparks of irritation, "I didn't come here to fight."

"Why are you here?"

"To bring you this."

She reached into her oversize, black leather bag and pulled out a legal-size manila envelope. Her fingers traced the silver clasp briefly as if she were hesitating about handing it over. Then a second later, she did.

Justice took it, glanced at it and asked, "What is it?"

"The divorce papers." She folded her arms across her chest. "You didn't sign the copy the lawyers sent you, so I thought I'd bring a set in person. Harder to ignore me if I'm standing right in front of you, don't you think?"

Justice tossed the envelope onto the nearest chair, stuffed his hands into the back pockets of his jeans and stared her down. "I wasn't ignoring you."

"Ah," she said with a sharp nod, "so you

were just what? Playing games? Trying to make me furious?"

He couldn't help the half smile that curved his mouth. "If I was, looks like I managed it."

"Damn right you did." She walked toward him and stopped just out of arm's reach. As if she knew if she came any closer, the heat between them would erupt into an inferno neither of them would survive.

He'd always said she was smart.

"Justice, you told me months ago that our marriage was over. So sign the damn papers already."

"What's your hurry?" The question popped out before he could call it back. Gritting his teeth, he just went with it and asked the question he really wanted the answer to. "Got some other guy lined up?"

She jerked her head back as if he'd slapped her.

"This is *not* about getting another man into my life," she told him. "This is about getting a man *out* of my life. You, Justice. We're not together. We're not going to be together. You made that plain enough."

"You leaving wasn't my idea," he countered.

"No, it was just your fault," she snapped.

"You're the one who packed, Maggie."

"You gave me no choice." Her voice broke and Justice hissed in a breath in response.

Shaking her head, she held up one hand as if for peace and whispered, "Let's just finish this, okay?"

"You think a signed paper will finish it?" He moved in, dragging his hands from his pockets so that he could grab her shoulders before she could skitter away. God, the feel of her under his hands again fed the cold, empty places inside him. Damn, he'd missed her.

"You finished it yourself, remember?"

"You're the one who walked out," Justice reminded her again.

"And you're the one who let me," she

snapped, her gaze locked on his as she stiffened in his grasp.

"What was I supposed to do?" he demanded. "Tie you to a chair?"

She laughed without humor. "No, you wouldn't do that, would you, Justice? You wouldn't try to make me stay. You wouldn't come after me."

Her words jabbed at him but he didn't say anything. Hell, no, he hadn't chased after her. He'd had his pride, hadn't he? What was he supposed to do, beg her to stay? She'd made it clear that as far as she was concerned, their marriage was over. So he should have done what exactly?

She flipped her hair back out of her face and gave him a glare that should have set him on fire. "So here we are again on the carousel of pain. I blame you. You blame me. I yell, you get all stoic and stone-faced and nothing changes."

He scowled at her. "I don't get stone-faced."

"Oh, please, Justice. You're doing it right

now." She choked out a laugh and tried to squirm free of his grip. It didn't work. She tipped her head back, and her angry eyes focused on his and the mouth he wanted to taste more than anything flattened into a grim slash. "Our fights were always one-sided. I shout and you close up."

"Shouting's supposed to be a good thing?"

"At least I would have known you cared enough to fight!"

His fingers on her shoulders tightened, and he met that furious glare with one of his own. "You knew damn well I cared. You still left."

"Because you had to have it all your way. A marriage is *two* people. Not just one really pushy person." She sucked in a breath, fought his grip for another second or two, then sighed. "Let me go, Justice."

"I already did," he told her. "You're the one who came back."

"I didn't come back for this." She pushed at his chest.

"Bullshit, Maggie." His voice dropped to a whisper, a rough scrape of sound as the words clawed their way out of his throat. "You could have sent your lawyer. Hell, you could have mailed the papers again. But you didn't. You came here. To *me*."

"To look you in the eye and demand that you sign them."

"Really?" He dipped his head, inhaled the soft, flowery scent of her and held it inside as long as he could. "Is that really why you're here, Maggie? The papers?"

"Yes," she said, closing her eyes, sliding her hands up his chest. "I want it over, Justice. If we're done, I need all of this to be finally over."

The feel of her touching Justice sparked the banked fires within and set them free to engulf his body. It had always been like this between them. Chemistry, pure and simple. Combustion. Whenever they touched, their bodies lit up like the neon streets of Vegas.

That, at least, hadn't changed.

"We'll never be done, Maggie." His gaze moved over her. He loved the flush in her cheeks and the way her mouth was parted on the sigh that slipped from between her lips. "What's between us will never be over."

"I used to believe that." Her eyes opened; she stared up at him and shook her head. "But it has to be over, Justice. If I stay, we'll only hurt each other again."

Undoubtedly. He couldn't give her the one thing she wanted, so he had to let her go. For her sake. Still, she was here, now. In his arms. And the past several months had been so long without her.

He'd tried to bury her memory with other women, but he hadn't been able to. Hadn't been able to want any woman as he wanted her. Only her.

His body was hard and tight and aching so badly it was all he could do not to groan with the pain of needing her. The past didn't matter anymore. The future was a hazy blur. But the present buzzed and burned with an intensity that shook him to his bones.

"If we're really done, then all we have is now, Maggie," he said, bending to touch the tip of his tongue to her parted lips. She hissed in a breath of air, and he knew she felt exactly as he did. "And if you leave now, you'll kill me."

She swayed into him even as she shook her head. Her hands slid up over his shoulder, and she drove her fingers up, into his always-too-long dark brown hair. The touch of her was molten. The scent of her was dizzying. The taste of her was all he needed.

"God, I've missed you," she admitted, her mouth moving against his. "You bastard, you've still got my heart."

"You ripped mine out when you left, Maggie," he confessed. His gaze locked with hers, and in those pale blue depths he read passion and need and all the emotions that were charging through him. "But you're back now and damned if I'll let you leave again. Not now. Not yet."

His mouth came down hard on hers, and it was as if he was alive again. For months, he'd been a walking dead man. A hollowed-out excuse for a human being. Breathing. Eating. Working. But so empty there was nothing for him but routine. He'd lost himself in the ranch workings. Buried himself in the minutiae of business so that he had no time to think. No time to wonder what she was doing. Where she was.

Months of being without her fired the desire nearly choking him, and Justice gave himself up to it. He skimmed his hands up and down her spine, sliding them over the curve of her bottom, cupping her, pressing her into him until she could feel the hard proof of his need.

She groaned into his mouth and strained against him. Justice tore his mouth from hers and lowered his head to taste the long, elegant line of her throat. Her scent invaded him. Her heat swamped him. And he could think only of taking what he'd wanted for so long.

He nibbled at her soft, smooth skin, feeling

her shivers of pleasure as she cocked her head to one side, allowing him greater access. She'd always liked it when he kissed her neck. When his teeth scraped her skin, when his tongue drew taut, damp circles just beneath her ear.

He slid one hand around, to the front of her. He cupped her center with the palm of his hand. Even through the fabric of her tailored slacks, he felt her heat, her need, pulsing at him.

"Justice…"

"Damn it, Maggie," he whispered, lifting his head to look down at her. "If you tell me to stop, I'll…"

She smiled. "You'll what?"

He sighed and let his forehead drop to hers. "I'll stop."

Maggie shifted her hold on him, moving to cup his face between her palms. She hadn't come here for this, though if she were to be completely honest, she'd have had to admit that she'd hoped he would hold her again. Love her again. She'd missed him so much that the pain of losing him was a constant ache in her heart. Now, having his hands and mouth on her again was like a surprise blessing from the suddenly benevolent fates.

When she'd first left him, she'd prayed that he'd follow her, take her home and make everything right. When he hadn't, it had broken her heart. But she'd tried to go on. To rebuild her life. She found a new job. Found an apartment. Made friends.

And still there was something missing.

A part of her she'd left here, at the ranch.

With him.

Looking up into the dark blue eyes that had captivated her from the first, she said, "Don't stop, Justice. Please don't stop."

He kissed her, hard and long and deep. His tongue pushed into her mouth, claiming her in a frenzy of passion so strong she felt the tide of it swamp her, threaten to drown her in an overload of sensation.

From the top of her head to the tips of her

toes, Maggie felt a rush of heat that was in-credible. As if she were literally on fire, she felt her skin burn, her blood boil and her heart thunder in her chest. While his mouth took hers, his clever fingers unzipped her slacks so that he could slide one hand down the front of her, beneath the fragile elastic of her panties to the swollen, hot flesh awaiting him.

She shivered as he stroked her intimately. She parted her legs for him, letting her slacks slide down to pool on the floor. She didn't care where they were. Didn't care about anything but feeling his hands on her again. Maggie nearly wept as he pushed first one finger and then two deep inside her.

Sucking in a gulp of air, she let her head fall back as she rode his hand, rocking her hips, seeking the release only he could give her. The passion she'd only ever found with him. She heard his own breath coming hard and fast as he continued to stroke her body inside and out. His thumb worked that so sensitive bud of flesh at the heart of her, and Maggie felt her brain sizzle as tension coiled inside her, tighter, tighter.

"Come for me, Maggie," he whispered. "Let me watch you shatter."

She couldn't have denied him even if she'd wanted to. It had been too long. She'd missed him too much. Maggie held on to his shoulders, fingers curling into the soft fabric of the long-sleeved shirt he wore, digging into his hard muscles.

Her mind spun, splintering with thoughts, images, while her body burned and spiraled even closer to its reward. She'd never felt anything like this with any man before him. And after Justice…she'd had no interest in other men. He was the one. She'd known it the moment she'd met him three years before. One look across a crowded dance floor at a charity event and she'd known. Instantly. It was as if everything in the world had held utterly still for one breathless moment.

Just like now.

There was nothing in the world but him and his hands. His touch. His scent. "Justice—I need…"

"I know, baby. I know just what you need. Take it. Take me." He touched her deeper, pushing his fingers inside her, stroking her until her breath strangled in her throat.

Until she could only groan and hold on to him. Until her body trembled and the incredible tension within shattered under an onslaught of pleasure so deep, so overwhelming, all she could do was shout his name as wave after wave of completion rolled over her, through her, leaving her dazed and breathless.

And when the tremors finally died away, Maggie stared up into Justice's lake-blue eyes and watched him smile. She was standing in the living room, with her pants down, trembling with the force of her reaction to him. She should have been…embarrassed. After all, anyone could have walked into the ranch house.

Instead, all Maggie felt was passion stirring inside again. His hands were talented, heaven knew. But she wanted more. She wanted the slide of Justice's body into hers.

Licking her lips, she blew out a breath and said, "That was…"

"…just the beginning," he finished for her.

Two

Sounded good to Maggie.

Yet… She glanced around the empty room before looking back at him. "Mrs. Carey's not here, but—"

"Nobody's here," he said quickly. "No one's coming. No one is going to interrupt us."

Maggie sighed in relief. She didn't want any interruptions. Justice was right about one thing—their past was gone. The future was gray and hazy. All she had was today. This minute. This one small slice of time, and she was going to relish every second of it.

Her fingers speared through his thick, soft hair, her nails dragging along his scalp. He always kept it too long, she thought idly, loving the way the dark brown mass lay across his collar. He had a day's worth of dark stubble on his jaws, and he looked so damned sexy he made her quiver.

Her breasts ached for his touch and as if he'd heard that stray thought, he pulled back from her slightly, just far enough so that his fingers could work the buttons on her pale pink silk blouse. Quickly, they fell free and then he was sliding the fabric off her shoulders to drop to the floor. She stepped out of her slacks, kicked off her half boots and slipped her lacy panties off.

Then he undid her bra, tossing it aside, and her breasts were free, his hands cupping her. His thumbs moved over her peaked nipples until she whimpered with the pleasure and the desire pumping fresh and new through her system. As if that climax hadn't even happened, her body was hot and trembling again.

Need crashed down on her, and at her core she ached and burned for him.

"You're beautiful," he whispered, drawing his mouth from hers, glancing down at her breasts, cupped in his palms. "So damn beautiful."

"I want you, Justice. Now. Please, now."

One corner of his mouth tipped into a wicked smile. His eyes flashed and in an instant he'd swept her up into his arms, stalked across the room and dropped her onto one of the wide sofas. She stared up at him as he tugged his shirt up and over his head. And her mouth watered. His skin, so tanned, so strong, so sculpted. God, she remembered all the nights she'd lain in his arms, held against that broad, warm chest. And she trembled at the rise of passion inside her.

She scooted back on the sofa until her head was resting on a pillow. Maggie held her arms out toward him. "What're you waiting for, cowboy?"

His eyes gleamed, his jaw went tight and hard. He finished undressing in a split second but still Maggie thought he was taking too long. She didn't want to wait. She was hot and wet and so ready for him that she thought she'd explode and die if he didn't take her soon.

He came to her and Maggie's gaze dipped to his erection, long and thick and hard. Her breath caught on a gasp of anticipation as Justice leaned down, tore the back cushions off the sofa and tossed them to the floor to make more room for them on the overstuffed couch. The dark green chenille fabric was soft and cool against her skin, but Maggie hardly noticed that slight chill. There was far too much heat simmering inside her, and when Justice covered her body with his, she could have sworn she felt actual flames sweeping over them.

"I've missed you, babe," he told her, bracing

himself on his hands, lowering his mouth to hers, tasting, nibbling.

"Oh, Justice, I've missed you, too." She lifted her hips for him, parting her thighs, welcoming him home. He pushed his body into hers with one hard stroke. She groaned, loving the long, deep slide of his flesh claiming hers. He filled her and she lifted her legs higher, hooking them around his waist, opening herself so that she could take him even deeper.

And still it wasn't enough. Wasn't nearly enough. She groaned, twisting and writhing beneath him as he moved in and out of her depths in plunging strokes that fanned the flames engulfing her.

It had been too long, she thought wildly. She didn't want soft and romantic. She wanted hard and fast and frantic. She wanted to know that he felt the same crushing need she did. She wanted to feel the strength of his passion.

"Harder, Justice," she whispered. "Take me harder."

He looked down at her and his eyes flashed. "I'm holding back, Maggie. It's been too long. I don't want to hurt you."

She cupped his face in her palms, fought to steady her breath and finally shook her head and smiled. "The only thing that hurts is when you hold back. Justice, I *need* you. All of you."

His jaw clenched tight, he swept one arm around her back, holding her to him even as he pushed off the couch. With their bodies locked together, her legs wrapped around his waist, he eased her onto the oriental carpet covering the hardwood floors. With her flat on her back, he levered himself over her, hands at either side of her head. Grinning down at her, he muttered, "Told you when you bought 'em those damn couches were too soft."

She grinned right back at him. "For sitting, they're perfect. For this…yeah. Too soft."

She lifted her hips then, taking him deeper inside. When he withdrew a moment later, she nearly groaned, but then he was back, driving himself into her, pistoning his hips against hers and she felt all of him. Took all of him. His need joined hers.

He lifted her legs, hooking them over his shoulders, tipping her hips higher so that he could delve even deeper, and Maggie groaned in appreciation. She slapped her hands onto the carpet and hung on as he moved faster and faster, driving them both to a shuddering climax that hovered just out of reach.

"Yes, Justice," she said, her voice nothing more than a strained hush of sound. "Just like that."

Again and again, his body claimed hers, pushing into her soft, hot folds, taking everything she offered and giving all that she could have wanted. She looked up into his eyes, saw the flash of something delicious wink in their depths and knew in that one blindingly clear instant that she would never be whole without him.

Without him.

That one random thought hovered at the edges of her mind and filled her eyes with tears even as her body began to sing and hum with the building tensions that rippled through her senses.

He touched her at their joining. Rubbing his thumb over that one spot that held so many incredible sensations. And as he touched her, Maggie hurtled eagerly toward the enormous climax waiting for her. As her body exploded with the force of completion, she screamed his name, and still she heard the quiet voice in the back of her mind whispering, *Is this our last time together?*

Then Justice gave himself over to his own release, her name an agonized groan sliding from his throat. When he collapsed atop her, Maggie held him close as the last of the tremors rippled through their joined bodies and eased them into oblivion.

And if her heart broke just a little, she wouldn't let him know it.

* * *

The rest of the weekend passed in a blurry haze of passion. But for a few necessary trips to the kitchen, Justice and Maggie never left the master bedroom.

After that first time in the living room, Justice made a call to his ranch manager, Phil, and told him to handle the ranch problems himself for the next few days. It hadn't exactly been a promise of forever, but Maggie had been happy for it.

All the same, she was crazy and she knew it. Setting herself up for another fall. As long as Justice King was the man she loved, she wasn't going to find any peace. Because they couldn't be together without causing each other pain and being apart was killing her.

How was that fair?

She sighed a little, her gaze still fixed on him. The only light in the room came from the river stone hearth, where a dying fire sputtered and flickered. Outside, a winter storm battered at the log mansion, tiny fists of rain tapping at the glass. And within Maggie, a different sort of storm raged.

What was she supposed to do? She'd tried living without him and had spent the most miserable nine months of her life. She'd tried to lose herself in her work, but it was an empty way to live. The sad truth was she wanted Justice. And without him, she'd never be really happy.

He was the most amazing lover she'd ever known. Every touch burned, every breath caressed, every whispered word was a promise of seduction that kept her hovering on the brink of a new climax no matter how many times he pushed her over the edge. Her skin hummed long after he stopped touching her. She closed her eyes and felt him inside her. Felt their hearts pounding in rhythm and couldn't help wondering, as she always had, how two people could be so close and so far apart at the same time.

Now she watched him get out of bed and walk naked across the bedroom. His body was long and lean and tanned from all the years of working in the sun. His dark brown hair hung past his shoulders. She'd always found that hair of his to be sexy as hell and what made it even sexier was that he was oblivious to just how good he looked. How dangerous. Her heartbeat quickened as her gaze moved over his back, and down over his butt. He moved with a stealthy grace that was completely innate. Everything about him was, she had to admit, fabulous. He was enough to make any woman toss her panties in the air and shout hallelujah. And she was no different.

He went into a crouch in front of the hearth. The fire was dying and he set a fresh log on the fading flames. Instantly the fire blazed into life, licking at the new wood, hissing and snapping.

Maggie watched Justice. His legs were muscled and toned from hours spent in a saddle. His back and shoulders were broad and sculpted from the hard work he never spared himself. As a King, he could have hired men to do the hard work around the ranch. But she knew it had always been a matter of pride to him that *he* be out there with those who worked for him.

Justice King was a man out of time, she thought, sweeping one arm across the empty space in the bed where he'd been lying only moments ago. He would have been completely at home in medieval times. He would have been a Highlander, she mused, her imagination dressing him in a war-torn plaid and placing a claymore in his fist.

As if he knew she was watching him, Justice turned his face to her, and the flickering light of the fire threw dancing shadows across his features. He looked hard and strong and suddenly so unapproachable that Maggie's heart gave a lurch.

She was setting herself up for pain and she knew it. He was her husband, but the bonds holding them together were frayed and tattered. In bed they were combustible and so damn good it made her heart hurt. It was when they were *out* of bed that things got complicated. They wanted different things. They each held so tightly to their own bottom line that compromise was unthinkable.

But it was Sunday night. The end of the weekend. She'd have to return to her world soon, and knowing that this time with him was nearly over was already bringing agonizing pain.

The storm blowing in off the coast howled outside the window. Rain hammered at the glass, wind whistled under the eaves and, Justice noticed, Maggie had started thinking.

Never had been a good thing, Justice told himself as he watched his wife study him. Whenever Maggie got that look on her face—an expression that said she had something to say he wasn't going to like—Justice knew trouble was coming.

But then, he'd been halfway prepared for that since this "lost" weekend had begun. Nothing had changed. He and Maggie, despite the obvious chemistry they shared, were still miles apart in the things that mattered, and great sex wasn't going to alter that any.

Her red-gold hair spilled across her pillow like hot silk. She held the dark blue sheet to her breasts even as she slid one creamy white leg free of the covers. She made a picture that engraved itself in Justice's mind, and he knew that no matter how long he lived, he would always see her as she was right at this moment.

He also knew that this last image of her would torment him forever.

"Justice," she said, "we have to talk."

"Why?" He stood up, crossed to the chair where he'd tossed his jeans and tugged them on. A man needed his pants on when he had a conversation with Maggie King.

"Don't."

He glanced at her. "Don't what?"

"Don't shut me out. Not this time. Not now."

"I'm not doing anything, Maggie."

"That's my point." She sat up, the mattress beneath her shifting a little with her movements.

Justice turned his head to look at her, and everything in him roared at him to stalk to her side, grab her and hold her so damn tight she wouldn't have the breath to start another argument neither of them could win.

Her hair tumbled around her shoulders, and she lifted one hand to impatiently push the mass behind her shoulders. "You're not going to ask me to stay, are you?"

He shouldn't have to, Justice told himself. She was his damn wife. Why should he have to ask her to be with him? She was the one who'd left.

He didn't say any of that, though, just shook his head and buttoned the fly of his jeans. He didn't speak again until his bare feet were braced wide apart. A man could lose his balance all too easily when talking to Maggie. "What good would it do to ask you to stay? Eventually, you'd leave again."

"I wouldn't have to if you'd bend a little."

"I won't bend on this," he assured her, though it cost him as he noted the flash of pain in her eyes that was there and then gone in a blink.

"Why not?" She pushed out of the bed, dropping the sheet and facing him, naked and proud.

His body hardened instantly, despite just how many times they'd made love over the past few hours. Seemed his dick was always ready when it came to Maggie.

"We are who we are," he told her, folding his arms across his chest. "You want kids. I don't. End of story."

Her mouth worked and he knew she was struggling not to shout and rail at him. But then, Maggie's hot Irish temper was one of the things that had first drawn him to her. She blazed like a sun during an argument—

standing her ground no matter who stood against her. He admired that trait even though it made him a little crazy sometimes.

"Damn it, Justice!" She stalked to the chair where she'd left her clothes and grabbed her bra and panties. Slipping them on, she shook her head and kept talking. "You're willing to give up what we have because you don't want a child?"

Irritation raced through him; he couldn't stop it. But he wasn't going to get into this argument again.

"I told you how I felt before we got married, Maggie," he reminded her, in a calm, patient tone he knew would drive her to distraction.

As expected, she whipped her hair back out of her eyes, glared at him fiercely, then picked up her pale pink blouse and put it on. While her fingers did up the buttons, she snapped, "Yes, but I just thought you didn't want kids that instant. I never thought you meant *ever.*"

"Your mistake," he said softly.

"But one you didn't bother to clear up," she countered.

"Maggie," he said tightly, "do we really have to do this again?"

"Why the hell not?" she demanded. Then pointing to the bed, she snapped, "We just spent an incredible weekend together, Justice. And you're telling me you feel *nothing?*"

He'd be a liar if he tried. But admitting what he was feeling still wouldn't change a thing. "I didn't say that."

"You didn't have to," she told him. "The very fact that you're willing to let me walk…*again*…tells me everything I need to know."

His back teeth ground together until he wouldn't have been surprised to find them nothing more than gritty powder in his mouth. She thought she knew him, thought she knew what he was doing and why, but she didn't have a clue. And never would, he reminded himself.

"Hell, Justice, you wouldn't back down even if you did change your mind, would you? Oh, no. Not Justice King. His pride motivates his every action—"

He inhaled deeply and folded his arms across his bare chest. "Maggie…"

She held up one hand to cut off whatever else he might say, and though he felt a kick to his own temper, he shut up and let her have her say.

"You know what? I'm sick to death of your pride, Justice. The great Justice King. Master of his Universe." She slapped both hands to her hips and lifted her chin. "You're so busy arranging the world to your specifications that there is absolutely no compromise in you."

"Why the hell should there be?" Justice took a half step toward her and stopped. Only because he knew if he got close enough to inhale her scent, he'd be lost again. He'd toss her back into the bed, bury himself inside her—and what would that solve? Not a thing. Sooner or later, they'd end up right here. Back at the fight that had finally finished their marriage.

"Because there were *two* of us in our marriage, Justice. Not just you."

"Right," he said with a brief, hard nod. He didn't like arguments. Didn't think they solved anything. If two people were far enough apart on an issue, then shouting at each other over it wasn't going to help any. But there was only just so much he was willing to take. "You want compromise? We each give a little? So how would you manage that here, Maggie? Have *half* a child?"

"Not funny at all, Justice." Maggie huffed out a breath. "You knew what family meant to me. What it still means to me."

"And you knew how I felt, too." Keeping his gaze steady and cool on hers, he said, "There's no compromise here, Maggie, and you know it. I can't give you what you want, and you can't be happy without it."

As if all the air had left her body, she slumped, the flash of temper gone only to be replaced by a well of defeat that glimmered in her eyes. And that tore at him. He hated seeing Maggie's spirit shattered. Hated even more that he was the one who'd caused it. But that couldn't be helped. Not now. Not ever.

"Fine," she said softly. "That's it, then. We end it. Again."

She picked up her slacks and put them on. Shaking her head, she zipped them up, tucked the tail of her shirt into the waistband and then stepped into her boots. Lifting her arms, she gathered up the tangle of her hair and deftly wound it into a knot at the back of her head, capturing that wild mass and hiding it away.

When she was finished, she stared at him for a long moment, and even from across the room Justice would have spared her this re-hashing of the argument that had finally torn them apart. But this weekend had proven to him as nothing else ever would, that the best thing he could do for her was to step back. Let her hate him if she had to. Better for her to move the hell on with her life.

Even if the thought of her moving on to another man was enough to carve his heart right out of his chest.

Maggie picked up her purse, slung it over her shoulder and stared at him. "So, I guess the only thing left to say is thanks for the weekend."

"Maggie…"

Shaking her head again, she started walking toward the door. When she came close to him, she stopped and looked up at him. "Sign the damn divorce papers, Justice."

She took another step and he stopped her with one hand on her arm. "It's pouring down rain out there. Why don't you stay put for a while and wait out the storm before you go."

Maggie pulled her arm free of his grasp and started walking again. "I can't stay here. Not another minute. Besides, we're not a couple, Justice. You don't have the right to worry about me anymore."

A few seconds later, he heard the front door slam. Justice walked to the windows and looked down on the yard. The wind tore her hair free of its tidy knot and sent long strands of red flying about her face. She was drenched by the rain almost instantly. She climbed into the car and fired up the engine. Justice saw the headlights come on, saw the rain slash in front of those twin beams and stood there in silence as she steered the car down the drive and off the ranch.

Chest tight, he watched until her taillights disappeared into the darkness. Then he punched his fist against the window and relished the pain.

Three

Justice threw his cane across the room and listened to it hit the far wall with a satisfying clatter. He hated needing the damn thing. Hated the fact that he was less than he used to be. Hated knowing that he needed help, and he sure as hell hated having his brother here to tell him so.

He glared at Jefferson, his eldest brother, then pushed up and out of the chair he was sitting in. Justice gathered up his pride and dignity and used every ounce of his will to make sure he hobbled only a little as he lurched from the chair to the window overlooking the front yard. Sunlight splashed through the glass into the room, bathing everything in a brilliant wash of light.

Justice narrowed his eyes at his brother, and when he was no more than a foot away from him, he stopped and said, "I told you I can walk. I don't need another damn therapist."

Jefferson shook his head and stuffed both hands into the pockets of what was probably a five-thousand-dollar suit. "You are the most stubborn jackass I've ever known. And being a member of this family, that's saying something."

"Very amusing," Justice told him and oh-so-casually shot out one hand to brace himself against the log wall. His knuckles were white with the effort to support himself and take the pressure off his bad leg. But he'd be damned if he'd show that weakness to Jefferson. "Now, get out."

"That's the attitude that ended up bringing me here."

"How's that?"

"You've chased off three physical therapists in the past month, Justice."

"I didn't bring 'em here," he pointed out.

Jefferson scowled at him, then sighed. "Dude, you broke your leg in three places. You've had surgery. The bones are healed but the muscles are weak. You need a physical therapist and you damn well know it."

"Don't call me 'dude,' and I'm getting along fine."

"Yeah, I can see that." Jefferson shot a quick glance to Justice's white-knuckled grip on the wall.

"Don't you have some inane movie to make somewhere?" Justice countered. As head of King Studios, Jefferson was the man in charge of the film division of the King empire. The man loved Hollywood. Loved traveling around the world, making deals, looking for talent, scouting locations himself. He was as footloose as Justice was rooted to this ranch.

"First I'm taking care of my idiot brother."

Justice leaned a little harder against the log wall. If Jefferson didn't leave soon, Justice was going to fall on his ass. Whether he wanted to admit it aloud or not, his healing leg was still too weak to be much good. And that irritated the hell out of him.

A stupid accident had caused all of this. His horse had stumbled into a gopher hole one fine morning a few months back. Justice had been thrown clear, but then the horse rolled across his leg, shattering it but good. The horse had recovered nicely. Justice, though, was having a tougher time. After surgery, he now carried enough metal in his bones to make getting through airport security a nightmare, and his muscles were now so flabby and weak it was all he could do to force himself to move.

"It's your own damn fault you're in this fix anyway," Jefferson said, as if reading Justice's mind. "If you'd been riding in a ranch jeep instead of sitting on top of your horse, this wouldn't have happened."

"Spoken like a man who's forgotten what it was like to ride herd."

"Damn right," Jefferson told him. "I put a lot of effort into forgetting about predawn rides to round up cattle. Or having to go and find a cow so dumb it got lost on its own home ranch."

This is why Jeff was the Hollywood mogul and Justice was the man on the ranch. His brothers had all bolted from the home ranch as soon as they were old enough, each of them chasing his own dream. But Justice's dreams were all here on this ranch. Here is where he felt most alive. Here, where the clear air and the open land could let a man breathe. He didn't mind the hard work. Hell, he relished it. And his brother knew why he'd been astride a horse.

"You grew up here, Jeff," he said. "You know damn well a horse is better for getting down into the canyons. And they don't have engines that scare the cattle and cause stress that will shut down milk production for the calves, not to mention running the jeeps on the grasslands only tears them up and—"

"Save it," Jeff interrupted, holding up both hands to stave off a lecture. "I heard it all from Dad, thanks."

"Fine, then. No more ranch talk. Just answer this." Justice reached down and idly rubbed at his aching leg. "Who asked you to butt into my life and start hiring physical therapists I don't even want?"

"Actually," Jefferson answered with a grin, "Jesse and Jericho asked me to. Mrs. Carey kept us posted on the situation with the therapists, and we all want you back on your feet."

He snorted. "Yeah? Why're you the only one here, then?"

Jefferson shrugged. "You know Jesse won't leave Bella alone right now. You'd think she was the only woman in the world to ever get pregnant."

Justice nodded, distracted from the argument at the moment by thoughts of their youngest brother. "True. You know he even sent me a book? *How to Be a Great Uncle*."

"He sent the same one to me and Jericho. Weird how he did this turnaround from wandering surfer to home-and-hearth expectant father."

Justice swallowed hard. He was glad for his brother, but he didn't want to think about Jesse's imminent fatherhood. Changing the subject, he asked, "So where's Jericho?"

"On leave," Jefferson told him. "If you'd open your e-mails once in a while, you'd know that. He's shipping out again soon, and he had some leave coming to him so he took it. He's soaking up some sun at cousin Rico's hotel in Mexico."

Jericho was a career marine. He loved the life and he was good at his job, but Justice hated that his brother was about to head back into harm's way. Why hadn't he been opening his e-mails? Truth? Because he'd been in a piss-poor mood since the accident. He should have known, though, that his brothers wouldn't just leave him alone in his misery.

"That's why you're here, then," Justice said. "You got the short straw."

"Pretty much."

"I should have been an only child," Justice muttered.

"Maybe in your next life," Jefferson told him, then pulled one hand free of his slacks pocket to check the time on his gold watch.

"If I'm keeping you," Justice answered with a bared teeth grin, "feel free to get the hell out."

"I've got time," his brother assured him. "I'm not leaving until the new therapist arrives and I can make sure you don't scare her off."

Wounded pride took a bite out of Justice and he practically snarled at his brother. "Why don't you all just leave me the hell alone? I didn't ask for your help and I don't want it. Just like I don't want these damn therapists moving in here like some kind of invasion."

He winced as his leg pained him, then finished by saying, "I'm not even gonna let this one in, Jeff. So you might as well head her off."

"Oh," Jefferson told him with a satisfied smile, "I think you'll let this one stay."

"You're wrong."

The doorbell rang just then and Justice heard his housekeeper's footsteps as she hustled along the hall toward the door. Something way too close to panic for Justice's own comfort rose up inside him. He shot Jefferson a quick look and said, "Just get rid of her, all right? I don't want help. I'll get back on my feet my own way."

"You've been doing it your own way for long enough, Justice," Jefferson told him. "You can hardly stand without sweat popping out on your forehead."

From a distance, Justice heard Mrs. Carey's voice, welcoming whoever had just arrived. He made another try at convincing his brother to take his latest attempt at help and leave.

"I want to do this on my own."

"That's how you do everything, you stubborn bastard. But everybody needs help sometimes, Justice," his brother said. "Even you."

"Damn it, Jefferson—"

The sound of two women's voices rippled through the house like music, rising and falling and finally dropping into hushed whispers. That couldn't be a good sign. Already his housekeeper was siding with the new therapist. Wasn't anyone loyal anymore? Justice scraped his free hand through his hair, then scrubbed his palm across his face.

He hated feeling out of control. And ever since his accident, that sensation had only been mounting. He'd had to trust in daily reports from his ranch manager rather than going out to ride his own land. He'd had to count on his housekeeper to take care of the tasks that needed doing around here. He wanted his damn life back, and he wasn't going to get it by depending on some stranger to come in and work on his leg.

He'd regain control only if he managed to come back from his injuries on his own. If that didn't make sense to anyone but him, well, he didn't care. This was *his* life, his ranch and, by God, he was going to do things the way he always had.

His way.

He heard someone coming and shot a sidelong glance at the open doorway, preparing himself to fire whoever it was the minute she walked in. His brothers could just butt the hell out of his life.

Footsteps sounded quick and light on the wood floor, and something inside Justice tightened. He had a weird feeling. There was no explanation for it, but for some reason his gut twisted into knots. Glancing at his brother, he muttered, "Just who the hell did you hire?"

Then a too-familiar voice announced from the doorway, "Me, Justice. He hired me."

Maggie.

His gaze shot to her, taking her in all at once as a man dying of thirst would near drown himself with his first taste of water. She was wearing blue jeans, black boots and a long-sleeved, green T-shirt. She looked curvier than he remembered, more lush somehow. Her hair was a tumble of wild curls around her shoulders and framing her face with fiery, silken strands. Her blue eyes were fixed on him and her mouth was curved into a half smile.

"Surprise," she said softly.

That about covered it, he thought. Surprise. Shock. Stunned stupid.

He was going to kill Jefferson first chance he got.

But for now he had to manage to stay on his feet long enough to convince Maggie that he didn't need her help. Damn it, she was the absolute last person in the world he wanted feeling sorry for him. Lifting his chin, he narrowed his gaze on her and said, "There's been a mistake, Maggie. I don't need you here, so you can go."

She flinched—actually flinched—and Justice felt like the bastard Jefferson had called him just a moment or two ago. But it was best for her to leave right away. He didn't want her here.

"Justice," his brother said in a long-suffering sigh.

"It's okay, Jeff," Maggie said, walking into the room, head held high, pale blue eyes glinting with the light of battle. "I'm more than used to your brother's crabby attitude."

"I'm not crabby."

"No," she said with a tight smile, "you're the very soul of congenial hospitality. I just feel all warm and fuzzy inside." Then she took a hard look at him. "Why are you standing?"

"What?"

Beside him, Jeff muffled a laugh and tried to disguise it with a cough. It didn't work.

"You heard me," Maggie said, rushing

across the room. When Justice didn't move, she grumbled something unintelligible, then dragged a chair over to him. She pushed him down onto it, and it was all Justice could do to hide the relief that getting off his feet gave him. "Honestly, Justice, don't you have any sense at all? You can't put all your weight on your bad leg or you'll be flat on your back again. Why aren't you using a cane at least?"

"Don't have one," he muttered.

"He threw it across the room," Jeff provided.

"Of course he did," Maggie said. She spotted the cane, then walked to retrieve it. When she came back to his side, she thrust it at him and ordered, "If you're going to stand, you're going to use the cane."

"I don't take orders from you, Maggie," he said.

"You do now."

"In case you didn't notice the lack of welcome, I'm firing you."

"You can't fire me," she told him, leaning

down to stare him dead in the eye. "Jefferson hired me. He's paying me to get you back on your feet."

"He had no right to." Justice sent his brother a hard glare, but Jefferson was rocking back and forth on his heels, clearly enjoying himself.

Maggie straightened up, fisted her hands at her hips and stared down at him with the stern look of a general about to order troops into battle. "He did hire me, though, Justice. Oh, and by the way, I've heard about the other three therapists who've come and gone from here—"

Justice looked past her to glare at his brother but looked back to Maggie again when she continued.

"—and you're not going to scare me off by throwing your cane. Or by being rude and nasty. So no need to try."

"I don't want you here."

"Yes," she said and a flicker of something sharp and sad shot through her eyes. "You've made that plain a number of times. But you can just suck it up. Because I'm here. And I'm staying. Until you can stand up without brackets of pain lining the sides of your mouth or gritting your teeth to keep from moaning. So you know what? Your best plan of action is to do exactly what I tell you to do."

"Why's that?"

"Because, Justice," she said, bracing her hands on the arms of his chair and leaning in until their faces were just a breath apart, "if you listen to me, you'll heal. And the sooner that happens, the sooner you'll get rid of me."

"Can't argue with her there," Jeff pointed out.

Justice didn't even glance at his brother. His gaze was locked with Maggie's. Her scent wafted to him like the scent of wildflowers on a summer wind. Her eyes shone with a silent challenge. Now that he was over the initial shock of seeing her walk into his life again, he could only hope to God she walked back out really soon.

Just being this close to her was torture. His

body was pressing against the thick denim fabric of his jeans. Good thing she'd pushed him into a chair so damn fast or she and his brother would have been all too aware of the kind of effect she had on him.

Maggie stared into Justice's eyes and felt her heart hammer in her chest. Seeing him again was like balm to an open wound. But seeing him hurt tore at her. So she was both relieved and miserable to be here.

Yet how could she have turned down Jefferson's request that she come to the ranch and help out? Justice was still her husband. Though he probably didn't realize that. No doubt he'd never even noticed that though he had signed the divorce papers and mailed them to her, she had never filed them with the courts. Naturally, even if he had noticed, Justice would have been too stubborn to call her and find out what was going on.

And as for Maggie? Well, she had had her own reasons for keeping quiet.

Strange. The last time she'd left this ranch, she'd been determined to sever the bond between her and Justice once and for all. But that plan had died soon enough when things had changed. Her life had taken a turn she hadn't expected. Hadn't planned for. A rush of something sweet and fulfilling swept through her and Maggie almost smiled. Nothing Justice did or said could make her regret what her life was now.

In fact, that was one of the reasons she'd come to help him, she told herself. Of course she would have come anyway, because she couldn't bear the thought of Justice being in pain and needing help he didn't have. But there was more. Maggie had leaped at Jefferson's request to come to the ranch, because she'd wanted the chance to show her husband what he was missing. To maybe open his stubborn eyes to the possibilities stretched out in front of him.

Now, though, as she stood right in front of

him and actually *watched* a shutter come down over his eyes, effectively blocking her out, she wondered if coming here had been the right thing to do after all.

Still, she *was* here. And since she was, she would at least get Justice back on his feet.

"So, what's it going to be, Justice?" she asked. "Going to play the tough, stoic cowboy? Or are you going to cooperate with me?"

"I didn't ask you to come," he told her, ignoring his brother standing just a foot or so away.

"Of course you didn't," Maggie retorted. "Everyone knows the great Justice King doesn't need anyone or anything. You're getting along fine, right?" She straightened up and took a step back. "So why don't you just get up out of that chair and walk me to the door."

His features tightened and his eyes flashed dangerously, and just for a second or two Maggie was half afraid he'd try to do just that and end up falling on his face. But the moment passed and he only glared at her. "Fine. You can stay."

"Wow." She placed one hand on her chest as if she were sighing in gratitude. "Thank you."

Justice glowered at her.

Jefferson cleared his throat and drew both of their gazes to him. "Well, then, looks like my work here is done. Justice, try not to be too big of an ass. Maggie," he said, moving to plant a quick kiss on her forehead, "best of luck."

Then he left and they were alone.

"Jefferson shouldn't have called you," Justice said quietly.

"Who else would he call?" Maggie looked at his white-knuckled grip on the cane he held in his right fist. He was angry, she knew. But more than that, he was frustrated. Her husband wasn't the kind of man to accept limitations in himself. Having to use a cane to support a weakened leg would gnaw at him. No wonder he was as charming as a mountain lion with its foot caught in a trap.

He blew out a breath. "I could get Mrs. Carey to throw you out."

Maggie laughed shortly. "She wouldn't do it. She likes me. Besides, you need me."

"I don't need your help or your pity. I can do this on my own."

A flare of indignation burst into life inside her. "That is so typical, Justice. You go through your life self-sufficient and expecting everyone else to do the same. Do it yourself or don't do it. That's your style."

"Nothing wrong with that," he argued. "A man's got to stand on his own."

"Why?" She threw both hands high and let them fall. "Why does it always have to be your way? Why can't you see that everyone needs someone else at *some* point?"

"I don't," he told her.

"Oh, no, not you. Not Justice King. You never ask for help. Never admit to needing anyone or anything. Heck, you've never even said the word *please.*"

"Why the hell should I?" he demanded.

"You're a hard man," Maggie said.

"Best you remember that."

"Fine. I'll remember." She stepped up close to him, helped him up from the chair despite his resistance and when he was standing, looked him dead in the eye and said, "As long as *you* remember that if you want to get your life back, you're going to have to take orders from me for a change."

Late that night Justice lay alone in the bed he used to share with his wife. He was exhausted, in pain and furious. He didn't want Maggie looking at him and seeing a patient. Yet, all afternoon she'd been with him, taking notes on his progress, telling him what he'd been doing wrong and then massaging his leg muscles with an impersonal competence that tore at him.

Every time she'd touched him, his body had reacted. He hadn't been able to hide his erection, but she'd ignored it—which infuriated him. It was as if he meant nothing to her. As if this were just a job.

Which it probably was.

Hell, what did he expect? They were divorced.

Grabbing the phone off the nightstand, he stabbed in a number from memory and waited impatiently while it rang. When his brother answered, Justice snapped, "Get her out of my house."

"No."

"Damn it, Jefferson," Justice raged quietly with a quick look at the closed door of his bedroom. For all he knew Maggie or Mrs. Carey was out wandering the hall, and he didn't want to be overheard. Which was the only thing that kept his voice low. "I don't want her here. I made my peace with her leaving, and having her here again only makes everything harder."

"Too bad," Jefferson shot back. "Justice, you need help whether you want to admit it or not. Maggie's a great therapist and you know it. She can get you back on your feet if you'll just swallow your damn pride and do what she tells you."

Justice hung up on his brother, but that didn't make him feel any better. *Swallow his pride?* Hell, his pride was all he had. It had gotten him through some tough times— watching Maggie walk out of his life, for instance—and damned if he was going to let it go now, when he needed it the most.

He scooted off the edge of the bed, too filled with frustration to try to sleep anyway. He could watch the flat-screen television he'd had installed a year ago, but he was too keyed up to sit still for a movie and too pissed off already to watch the news.

Disgusted by the need for it, Justice reached for his cane and pried himself off the mattress, using the thickly carved oak stick for balance. His injured leg ached like a bad tooth, and that only served to feed the irritation already clawing at his insides. Shaking his head, he hobbled toward the window but stopped dead when he heard…something.

Frowning, he turned toward the doorway and the hall beyond. He waited for that noise to come again, and when it did, his scowl deepened. What the hell?

He made his way to the door, flung it open and stood on the threshold, glancing up and down the hallway. The wall sconces were lit, throwing golden light over the narrow, dark red-and-green carpet, which lay like a path down the polished oak floors. The hallway was empty, and yet…

There it was again.

Sounded like a cat mewling. Justice moved toward the sound with slow, uncertain steps. Just one more reason to hate his damn cane and his own leg for betraying him. A few months ago he'd have stalked down this hallway with long strides. Now he was reduced to an ungainly stagger.

He followed the sound to the last door at the end of the hallway. The room Maggie was to stay in while she was on the ranch. At least he'd been able to order *that* much. He'd wanted her as far from his bedroom as possible to avoid the inevitable temptation.

Outside her door he cocked his head and listened. The house made its usual groaning noises as night settled in and the temperature dropped. Seconds ticked past and then he heard it again. That soft, wailing sound that he couldn't quite place. Was she crying? Missing him? Regretting coming to the ranch?

He should knock, he told himself. But if he did and she told him to go away, he'd have to. So instead, Justice turned the knob, threw open the door and felt the world fall out from beneath his feet.

Maggie.

Holding a baby.

She looked up at him and smiled. "Hello, Justice. I'd like you to meet Jonas. My son."

Four

"**W**hat? Who? How? What?" Justice jolted back a step, hit the doorjamb and simply stared at the woman and baby on the wide, king-size bed.

Maggie's gaze locked on his as she answered his questions in order. "My son. Jonas. The usual way. And again, my son."

Pain like Justice had never known before shot through him with a swiftness that stole his breath and nearly knocked him off his feet.

Maggie had a son.

Which meant she had a lover.

She was with someone else.

Everything in him went cold and hard. Amazing, really, how big the pain was. He'd told himself he was over her. Assured himself that their marriage was done and that it was for the best. For both of them. Yet now, when he was slapped with the proof that what they'd shared was over, the sharp stab of regret was hard enough to steal his breath. The thought of Maggie lying in another man's arms almost killed him. But then, what had he expected? That they'd get a divorce and she'd join a convent? Not his Maggie. She had too much fire.

Clearly, it hadn't taken her too long to move on. Her son looked to be several months old, which meant that she'd rolled out of his bed into someone else's real damn fast. Which made him wonder whether she'd been involved with someone else already when they'd had that last weekend together. That thought chewed on Justice, too. All the time they'd been rolling around in his bed, she'd had another guy waiting for her? What the hell was up with that?

He wanted to shout. To rage. But he didn't. He locked up everything inside him and refused to let her see that he was affected at all. Damned if he'd give her the satisfaction of knowing that she still had the power to cut him.

He had his pride, after all.

"Not going to say anything else?" she asked, swinging her legs off the bed and lifting the baby to sit at her hip.

He wiped one hand across his whiskered jaw and fought for indifference. "What do you want me to say? Congratulations? Fine. I said it." His gaze stayed locked on hers. He wouldn't look at the chubby-cheeked infant making insensible noises and gurgles.

"Don't you want to know who his father is?" she asked, moving closer with small, deliberate steps.

Why the hell was she doing this? Did she really enjoy rubbing the fact of her new relationship in his face? He hoped she was enjoying the show because, yeah, he did want to know. Then he wanted to find the guy and beat the crap out of him. But that wasn't going to happen. "None of my business, is it?"

"Actually, yes," she said, turning her head to plant a kiss on the baby's brow before looking back at Justice. "It sort of is. Especially since *you're* his father."

Another jolt went through Justice, and he wondered idly how many lightning strikes a man could survive in one night. Whatever game she was trying to run wouldn't work. She didn't have any way of knowing it, of course, but there was no possible way he was that baby's father.

So why the hell would she lie? Was the real father not interested in his kid? Is that why Maggie sought to convince Justice that he was the father instead? Or was it about money? Maybe she was trying to get some child support out of this. That would be stupid, though. All it would take was a paternity test and they'd all know the truth.

Maggie wasn't a fool. Which brought him right back to the question at hand.

What was she up to?

And why?

He stared at her, reading a challenge in her eyes. He still couldn't bring himself to look at the child. It was there, though, in his peripheral vision. A babbling, chortling statement on Justice's failure as a husband and Maggie's desire for family, provided by some other guy.

Pain grabbed at him again, making the constant ache in his leg seem like nothing more substantial than a stubbed toe.

"Nice try," he said, fixing his gaze on her with a cold distance he hoped was easily read.

"What's that mean?"

"It means, Maggie, I'm *not* his father, so don't bother trying to pawn him off on me."

"Pawn him—" She stopped speaking, gulped in air and tightened her hold on the baby, who was slapping tiny fists against her shoulder. "That's not what I'm trying to do."

"Really?" Justice swallowed past the knot in his throat and managed to give her a tight smile that was more of a baring of his teeth than anything else. "Then why is he here?"

"Because I am, you dolt!" Maggie took another step closer to him, and Justice forced himself to hold his ground. With the weakness in his leg, if he tried to step back, he might just go down on his ass, and wouldn't that be a fine end to an already spectacular day?

"I'm his mother," Maggie told him. "He goes where I go. And I thought maybe his daddy would like a look at him."

One more twist of the knife into his gut. He hadn't been able to give her the one thing she'd really wanted from him. Now seeing her with the child she used to dream of was torture. Especially since she was looking into his eyes and lying.

"I'm not buying it, Maggie, so just drop it, all right? I'm not that kid's father. I'm not anybody's father. So why the song and dance?"

"How can you know you're not?" she argued, clearly willing to stick to whatever game plan she'd had in mind when she got here. "Look at Jonas. Look at him! He has your eyes, Justice. He has your hair. Heck, he's even as stubborn as you are."

As if to prove her point, the baby gave up slapping at her shoulder for attention, reached out and grabbed hold of Maggie's gold, dangling earring. He gave it a tug, squealing in a high-pitched tone that made Justice wince. Gently, Maggie pried that tiny fist off her earring and gave her son a bright smile.

"Don't pull, sweetie," she murmured, and her son cooed at her in delight.

That softness in her voice, the love shining in her eyes, got to him as nothing else could have. Justice swallowed hard and finally forced himself to look at the child. Bright red cheeks, sparkling dark blue eyes and a thatch of black hair. He wore a diaper and a black T-shirt that read Cowboy in Training and was waving and kicking his chubby arms and legs.

Something inside him shifted. If he and Maggie had been able to have children, this is just what he would have expected their child to look like. Maybe that's why she thought her ploy would work on him. The kid looked enough like Justice that she probably thought she could convince him he was the father and then talk him out of a paternity test.

Sure. Why would she think he'd insist on that anyway? They had been married. The timing for the child was about right. She'd have no reason to think that he wouldn't believe her claims. But that meant that whoever had fathered the boy had turned his back on them. Which, weirdly, pissed him off on Maggie's behalf. What the hell kind of man would do that to her? Or to the baby? Who wouldn't claim his own child?

He watched the boy bouncing up and down on Maggie's hip, laughing and drooling, and told himself that if there were even the slightest chance the boy was actually his, Justice would do everything in his power to take care of him. But he knew the truth, even if Maggie didn't.

"He's a good-looking boy."

Maggie melted. "Thank you."

"But he's not mine."

She wanted to argue. He could see it in her face. Hell, he knew her well enough to know that there was nothing Maggie liked more than a good argument. But this one she'd lose before she even started.

He couldn't be Jonas's father. Ten years before, Justice had been in a vicious car accident. His injuries were severe enough to keep him in a hospital for weeks. And during his stay and the interminable testing that was done, a doctor had told him that the accident had left him unlikely to ever father children.

The doctor had used all sorts of complicated medical terms to describe his condition, but the upshot was that Jonas couldn't be his. Maggie had no way of knowing that, of course, since Justice had never told anyone about the doctor's prognosis. Not even his brothers.

Before he and Maggie got married, when she started talking about having a family, he'd told her that he didn't want kids. Better to let her believe he chose to remain childless rather than have her think he was less than a man.

His spine stiffened as that thought scuttled through his brain. He hadn't told her the truth then and he wouldn't now. Damned if he'd see a flash of pity in her eyes for him. Bad enough that she was here to see him struggle to do something as simple as *walk*.

"So who were you with, Maggie?" he asked,

his voice a low and dark hum. "Why didn't he want his kid?"

"I was with *you,* you big jerk," she said tightly. "I didn't tell you about the baby before because I assumed from everything you'd said that you wouldn't want to know."

"What's changed, then?" he asked.

"I'm here, Justice. I came here to help you. And I decided that no matter what, you had the right to know about Jonas."

If it were possible, Maggie would have said that Justice's features went even harder. But what was harder than stone? His eyes were flat and dark. His jaw was clenched. He was doing what he always had done. Shutting down. Shutting her out. But why?

Yes, she knew he'd said he didn't want children, but she'd been so sure that the moment he saw his son, he'd feel differently. That Jonas would melt away his father's reservations about having a family.

She'd even, in her wildest fantasies,

imagined Justice admitting he was wrong for the first time in his life. In her little dream world, Justice had taken one look at his son, then begged Maggie's forgiveness and asked her to stay, to let them be a family. She should have known better. "Idiot."

"I'm not an idiot," he told her.

"I wasn't talking to you," she countered. He was so close to her and yet so very far away.

The house was quiet, tucked in for the night. Outside the windows was the moonlit darkness, the ever-present sea wind blowing, rattling the windowpanes and sending tree branches scratching against the roof.

Justice stood not a foot from her, close enough that she felt the heat of his body reaching out for her. Close enough that she wanted to lean into him and touch him as she'd wanted to during the therapeutic massage she'd given him earlier.

Instantly, warmth spiraled through her as she remembered his response to her hands moving on the weakened muscles in his leg.

His erection hadn't been weak, though, and hadn't been easy to ignore, especially since being near him only made her want the big dummy more than ever.

"Look," Justice muttered, breaking the spell holding Maggie in place, "I'm willing to do the therapy routine. I don't like it, but I need to get back on my feet. If you can help with that, great. But if you staying here is gonna work, you're going to have to drop all of this crap about me being your baby's father. I don't want to hear it again."

"So you want me to lie," she said.

"I want you to stop lying."

"Fine. No lies. You are Jonas's father."

He gritted his teeth and muttered, "Damn it, Maggie!"

"Don't you swear in front of my son." She glanced at Jonas and though he was only six months old, she could see that he was confused and worried about what was happening. His big eyes looked watery, and his lower lip trembled as if he were getting ready to let a wail loose.

Justice barked out a harsh laugh. "You think he understood that?"

She glanced at the baby's big blue eyes, so much like his father's, and stroked a fingertip along his jaw soothingly. "I think he understands tone," she said quietly. "And I don't want you using that tone in front of him."

He blew out a breath, scowled ferociously for a second, then said, "Fine. I won't cuss in front of the kid. But you quit playing games."

"I'm not playing."

"You're doing something, Maggie, and I can tell you now, it's not going to work."

She stared up at him and shook her head. "I knew you were stubborn, Justice, but I never imagined you could be *this* thick-headed."

"And I never figured you for a cheat." He turned and started to painstakingly make his way out of the room into the hall.

Just for a second she watched him walk

away and her heart ached at the difficulty he had. Seeing a man as strong and independent as Justice leaning on a cane tore at her. His injuries weren't permanent, but she knew what it was costing his pride to haltingly move away from her.

But though she felt for him, she wasn't about to let him get away with what he'd just said.

"*Cheat?* A cheat?" Maggie inhaled sharply, cast another guilty glance at her son and gave him a smile she didn't feel. She wouldn't upset her baby for the sake of a man who was so blind he couldn't see the truth when it was staring him in the face. "I am not a cheat or a liar, Justice King."

He didn't look back at her. He just kept moving awkwardly down the hall, his cane tapping against the floor runner. If his plan was to escape her, he'd have to be able to move a lot faster than that, Maggie told herself. Quickly, she walked down the hall, stepped out in front of him and forced him to stop.

"Get out of the way," he murmured, staring past her, down the hall at his open bedroom door.

"You can think whatever you like of me, but you will, by God, not ignore me," she told him, and the fact that he kept avoiding meeting her eyes only further infuriated her. This had so not gone the way she'd hoped and expected.

When Jefferson called her, asking her to come help Justice, she'd taken it as a sign. That this was the way they would come together again. That the time was finally right for Justice to meet the son he didn't know about. Apparently, she had been wrong.

"Are you too cowardly to even look at me?" she demanded, knowing that the charge of coward would get his attention.

Instantly, he turned his dark blue gaze on her and she saw carefully banked anger simmering up from their depths. Well, good. At least he was feeling *something*.

"Don't push me, Maggie. For both our sakes. If you want me to watch my tone around your son, then don't you push me."

He was furious—she could see that. But beyond the anger there was hurt. And that tore at her. He didn't have to be hurt, darn it. She was offering him their son, not the plague.

"Justice," she said softly, smoothing one hand up and down her baby's back, "you know me better than anyone. You know I wouldn't lie to you about this. You are my son's father."

He snorted.

Insulted and stung by his obvious distrust, she stepped back from him. How could he believe that she was lying? How could he have ever claimed to love her and *not* know that she was incapable of trying to trick him in this way? What the hell kind of a husband was he, anyway?

"I'm trying to be understanding," she said, but her temper simmered just beneath the words. "I know this is probably all a surprise."

"You could say that."

"But I'm not going to say it to you again. I won't argue. I won't force you to admit your responsibilities—"

"I always face my responsibilities, Maggie. You should know that."

"And you should know I'm not a liar."

He blew out a breath, cocked his head to one side and stared into her eyes. "So what? We call it a draw? A standoff? An armed truce?"

"Call it whatever you want, Justice," Maggie said, before he could say something else that would hurt her. "All I'm going to say is that if you don't believe me about Jonas, then it's your loss, Justice. We created a beautiful, healthy son together. And I love him enough for both of us."

"Maggie…"

She placed one hand on the back of her son's head, holding him to her tenderly. "And in case you were wondering why I waited until now to tell you about Jonas… It's because I was worried about how you'd react." She laughed shortly, sharply. "Imagine that. Wonder why?"

He muttered something under his breath, and judging by the expression on his face, she was just as happy she'd missed it.

"The sad truth is, Justice, I never wanted my son to know that his own father hadn't wanted him."

His eyes went colder, harder than before, and Maggie shivered a little under his direct gaze. A second passed, then two, and neither of them spoke. The hall light was soft and golden, throwing delicate shadows around the wide, empty passage. They were alone in the world, the three of them, with an invisible and apparently impenetrable wall separating Maggie and her son from the man who should have welcomed them with open arms.

At last, Justice turned his gaze to the boy who was watching him curiously. Maggie watched her husband's features soften briefly before freezing up into that hardened, take-no-prisoners expression she knew so well. After several long moments he lifted his gaze to hers, and when he spoke, his voice was so soft she had to hold her breath to hear him.

"You're wrong, Maggie. If I *was* his father, I would want him."

Then he brushed past her, the tip of his cane making a muffled thumping sound as he made his way to his room. He didn't look back.

And that nearly broke Maggie's heart.

Five

"**R**un the calves and their mamas to the seaward pasture," Justice told Phil, his ranch manager, three days later. "You can leave the young bulls in the canyons for now. Keep them away from the heifers as much as you can."

"I know, boss." Phil turned the brim of his hat between his hands as he stood opposite the massive desk in Justice's study.

Phil was in his early fifties, with a tall, lanky body that belied his strength. He was a no-BS kind of guy who knew his job and loved the ranch almost as much as his boss. Phil's face was tanned as hard and craggy as leather from years spent in the sun. His forehead, though, was a good two shades lighter than the rest of him, since his hat was usually on and pulled down low. He shifted uneasily from foot to foot, as if eager to get outside and back on his horse.

"We've got most of the herd settled into their pastures now," he said. "There was a fence break in the north field, but two of the boys are out there now fixing it."

"Okay." Justice tapped a pen against the top of his desk and tried to focus the useless energy burning inside him. Sitting behind a desk was making him itchy. If things were as they should be, he'd be out on his own horse right now. Making sure things were getting done to his specifications. Justice wasn't a man to sit inside and order his people around. He preferred having his hand in everything that went on at King Ranch.

Phil Hawkins was a good manager, but he wasn't the boss.

Yet even as he thought it, Justice knew he was lying to himself. His itchy feeling had nothing to do with not trusting his crew. It was all about how he hated being trapped in the damn house. Now more than ever.

The past few days, he'd felt as if he was being stalked. Maggie was following him around, insisting on therapy sessions or swims in the heated pool or nagging at him to use the damn cane he'd come to hate. Hell, he'd had to sneak away just to get a few minutes alone in his office to go over ranch business with Phil.

Everywhere he went, it seemed, there was Maggie. Back in the day, they'd have been falling into each other's arms every other minute. But nothing was as it had once been. These days, she looked at him as if he were just another patient to her. Someone to feel bad for. To fix up. To take care of.

Well, he didn't need taking care of. Or if he

did, he'd never admit it. He didn't want her being *paid* to be here. Didn't want to be her latest mission. Her cause. Didn't want her touching him with indifference.

That angry thought flashed through his mind at the same time a twinge of pain sliced at his leg. Damn thing was near useless. And three days of Maggie's torture hadn't brought him any closer to healing and getting on with his life. Instead, she seemed to be settling in. Making herself comfortable in the log house that used to be her home.

She was sliding into the rhythm of ranch life as if she'd never left it. She was up with the dawn every day and blast if it didn't seem she was deliberately close enough to him every morning so that Justice heard her talking to her son. Heard the baby's nonsensical prattle and cooing noises. Could listen in on what he wasn't a part of.

She was everywhere. Her or the baby. Or both. He heard her laughing with Mrs. Carey, smelled her perfume in every room of the house and caught her playing with her son on several occasions. She and the baby had completely taken over his house.

There were toys scattered everywhere, a walker with bells, whistles and electronic voices singing out an alphabet song. There was a squawking chicken, a squeaky dog and a teddy bear with a weird, tinny voice that sang songs about sharing and caring. Hell, coming down the stairs this morning, he'd almost killed himself when his cane had come down on a ball with a clown's face stamped on it. There were cloth books, cardboard books and diapers stashed everywhere just in case the kid needed a change. That boy had to go through a hundred of them a day. And what was with all the books? It was not as if the baby could read.

"Uh, boss?"

"What?" Justice shook his head, rubbed at his aching leg and shifted his gaze back to Phil. That woman was now sneaking into his thoughts so that he couldn't even *talk* about ranch business. "Sorry," he said. "My mind wandered. What?"

Phil's lips twitched as if he knew where his boss's mind had slipped off to. But he was smart enough not to say anything. "The new grasses in the east field are coming in fine, just like you said they would. Looks like a winner to me."

"That's good news," Justice said absent-mindedly. They'd replanted one of the pastures with a hardier stock of field grass, and if it held up to its hype, then the herd would have something to look forward to in a few months.

Running an organic cattle ranch was more work, but Justice was convinced it was worth it in the long run. The cowboys he had working for him spent most of their time switching the cattle around to different pastures, keeping the grass fresh and the animals on the move. His cows didn't stand in dirty stalls to be force-fed grains. King cattle roamed open fields as they'd been meant to.

Cattle weren't born to eat corn, for God's sake. They were grazers. And keeping his herds moving across natural field grasses made the meat more tender and sweet and brought higher prices from the consumer. He had almost sixty thousand acres of prime grassland here on the coast and another forty thousand running alongside his cousin Adam's ranch in central California.

Justice had made the change over to natural grazing and organic ranching nearly ten years ago, as soon as he took over the day-to-day running of King Ranch. His father hadn't put much stock in it, but Justice had been determined to run the outfit his way. And in that time, he'd been able to expand and even open his own online beef operation.

He only wished his father had lived to see what he'd made of the place. But his parents had died in the same accident that had claimed Justice's chances of ever making his own family. So he had to content himself with knowing that he'd made a success of the family spread and that his father would have been proud.

"Oh, and we got another offer on Caleb," Phil was saying, and Justice focused on the man.

"What was it?"

"Thirty-five thousand."

"No," Justice told him. "Caleb's too valuable a stud to let him go for that. If the would-be buyer wants to pay for calves out of Caleb, we'll do that. But we're not selling our top breeding bull."

Phil grinned. "That's what I told him."

Some of Justice's competitors were more convinced it was his breeding stock that made his cattle so much better than others, and they were continually trying to buy bulls. They were either too stupid or too lazy to realize that fresh calves weren't going to change anything. To get the results Justice had, they were going to have to redo their operations completely.

The door to the study swung open after a perfunctory knock, and both men turned to look. Maggie stood in the open doorway. Faded jeans clung to her legs and the King Cattle T-shirt she wore in bright blue made her eyes shine like sapphires. She gave Phil a big smile. "You guys finished?"

"Yes, ma'am," Phil said.

"No," Justice said.

His ranch manager winced a little as he realized that he'd blown things for his boss.

Maggie looked at her husband. "Which is it? Yes or no?"

Frowning, Justice scowled at his foreman, silently calling him *traitor.* Phil just shrugged, though, as if to say it was too late now.

"We're finished for the time being," Justice reluctantly admitted.

"Good. Time for your exercises," Maggie told him, walking into the room and heading for his desk.

"Then I'll just go—" Phil waved his hat in

the direction of the door "—back to work." He nodded at her. "Maggie, good to see you."

"You, too," she said, giving the other man the kind of brilliant smile that Justice hadn't seen directed at him in far too long.

"He hasn't changed at all," Maggie mused.

"You haven't been gone that long."

"Funny," she said, "feels like a lifetime to me."

"I guess it would." Justice didn't want her in here. This was his office. His retreat. The one room in the whole place that hadn't been colored by her scent. By her presence. But it was too late now.

As she wandered the room, running her fingertips across the leather spines of the books in the shelves, he told himself that from now on, he'd see her here. He'd feel her here. He'd be able to close his eyes and imagine her with him, the sound of her voice, the sway of her hips, the way the sunlight through the window made her hair shine like a fire at midnight.

Squirming uncomfortably in his chair now,

Justice said, "You know, if you don't mind, I've got some paperwork to catch up on. Things pile up if you don't stay on top of them. Think I'll skip the exercises this morning."

She gave him the sort of smile she would have given a little boy trying to get away with cutting school. "I don't think so. But if you want, we can change things up a little. Instead of a half hour on the treadmill, we could walk around the ranch yard."

Sounded like a plan to him. He hated that damn treadmill with a raging passion. What the hell good was it, when a man had the whole world to walk in? Who would choose to walk on a conveyor belt? And if she didn't have him on that treadmill, she had him doing lunges and squats, with his back up against the wall. He felt like a lab rat, moving from one maze to the next. Always inside. Always moving and getting exactly nowhere.

The thought of getting outside was a blessing. Outside. Into the air, where her perfume would get lost in the wind rather than clinging to every breath he took. "Fine."

He pushed up from his black leather chair, and as he stepped around the edge of the desk, Maggie approached and held out his cane. He took it, his fingers brushing against hers just enough to kindle a brand-new fire in his gut. He pulled back, tightened his grip on the head of the blasted cane and started for the door.

"You're walking easier," she noted.

Irritation spiked inside him. He remembered a time when she had watched his ass for a different reason. "Yeah," he admitted. "It still hurts like a bitch, but maybe it's a little better."

"Wow. Quite the compliment to my skills."

He stopped and turned to look at her. "Maybe I'm doing well enough to just cut the therapy short."

"Ooh, good effort," she said and walked past him toward the front door.

Now it was his turn to watch her ass, and he for damn sure wasn't doing it to check out her ability to walk. Then something struck him: the fact that she didn't have her son on her hip. "Uh, don't you have to watch…"

"Jonas?" she provided.

"Yeah."

"Mrs. Carey has him. She loves watching him," Maggie said, striding down the hall to the front door. Her boots, which clacked against the wood floor, sounded like a quickening heartbeat. "Says he reminds her so much of you it's almost eerie."

Justice scowled at her back. She managed to get one or two of those pointed digs in every day. Trying to make him see something that wasn't there. A connection between her son and him.

He should just tell her, he thought, snatching his battered gray felt hat off the hook by the door. Tell her that he was sterile and be done with it. Then she could stop playing whatever game she was playing and he wouldn't have to put up with any of this anymore.

But if he did that, she'd know. Know everything. Why he'd let her go. Why he'd lied. Why he felt less than a man because he hadn't been able to give her the one thing she'd wanted. And, damn it, once he told her the truth, she'd feel sorry for him—and he couldn't stand that. Better for him if she thought him a bastard.

Maggie listened to the uncertain steps of her husband coming up behind her and stopped on the porch to wait for him. She took that moment to admire the sweep of land stretching out in front of her. She'd missed this place almost as much as she'd missed Justice. The wide yard was neatly tended, the flower beds were spilling over with bright, colorful blossoms and from somewhere close by, the lowing of a cow sounded almost like a song.

Just for a second or two, all of Maggie's thoughts and worries drifted away, just drained out of her system as if they'd never been there. She took a deep breath of the sweet air and smiled at two herd dogs, a mutt and a Lab, chasing each other across the front yard. Then she sensed Justice coming up behind her, and in an instant tension coiled deep in the pit of her stomach.

She would always sense him. Always be aware of him on a deep, cellular level. He touched something inside her that no one else ever had. And when they were apart, she felt his absence keenly. But feeling connected to a man who clearly didn't share the sentiment was just a recipe for disaster.

"It's really beautiful," she whispered.

"It is."

His deep voice rumbled along her spine and tingled through her system. Why did it have to be *him* who did this to her? she wondered and glanced over her shoulder at him. He wasn't looking at the ranch; he was watching her, and her knees went a little wobbly. Maggie had to lock them just to keep upright. The man's eyes should be illegal. His smile was even more lethal—thank heaven she didn't see it often.

"You used to love it here," he said quietly, letting his gaze slide from her to where the dogs chased each other in dizzying circles.

"I did," she admitted and took a deep breath.

From the moment she had first seen this ranch, it had felt like home to her. As if it had only been waiting for her to arrive, the ranch had welcomed her. Maggie had always been amazed that she could stand on her porch and feel as though she were in the middle of the country, when in reality the city was just a short freeway ride away.

Here on the King Ranch it was as if time had not exactly stood still but at least had taken a break, slowed down. She'd always thought this would be a perfect place for her children to grow up. She'd imagined watching four or five King kids racing through the yard laughing, running to her and Justice for hugs and kisses and growing up learning to care for the ranch as much as their father did.

But those dreams had died the night she'd left Justice so many months ago.

Now she was nothing more than a barely tolerated visitor, and Jonas would never know what it was like to grow up among his father's memories.

Or to grow up with his father's love.

Justice was deliberately closing himself off from not only her but also the child they'd made together. That was something she couldn't forgive. Or understand. Justice had always been a hard man, but he was also a man devoted to family. To his brothers and the King heritage. So how could he turn his back on his own son?

In the past three days, Justice had done everything in his power to avoid so much as being in the same room with Jonas. Her heart twisted painfully in her chest, but she wouldn't *force* him to care, even if she could.

Because then his love wouldn't mean a thing. To her or her son. So she would be professional and keep her emotions tightly leashed if it killed her.

"Loving this place didn't keep you here," he pointed out unnecessarily.

"No, it didn't," she said. "It couldn't."

He shook his head and frowned, squinting out from beneath the brim of his hat. "It could have. You chose to leave."

"I'm not going over that same old argument again, Justice."

"Me neither," he said with a shrug. "I'm just reminding you."

Maggie inhaled slowly, deeply. She told herself to bank her temper, to not let him get to her. It wasn't easy, especially since Justice had always known exactly which of her buttons to push to get a reaction. But as satisfying as it would be to shout and rage and give in to her frustration by telling him just what she was thinking, it wouldn't do a darn bit of good.

"We should walk." She spoke up fast, before her temper could override her more rational side. Then she turned to offer him her arm so she could assist him getting down the short flight of steps leading from the porch to the yard.

Instantly, he scowled at her and stepped around her, the tip of his cane slamming down onto the porch. "I'm not completely helpless, Maggie. I can get around without holding on to your arm. You're half my size."

"And trained to help ambulatory patients get around. I'm stronger than I look, Justice. You should remember that."

He shot her one hard, stony glare. "I'm not one of your patients, damn it."

"Well, yeah," she countered, feeling the first threads of her patience begin to unravel, "technically, you are."

"I don't want to be—don't you get that?"

She felt the cold of his stare slice right into her, but Maggie had practice in facing down his crab-ass attitude. "Yes, Justice. I get it.

Despite the great trouble you've taken in trying to hide how you feel about me being here, I get it."

His mouth flattened into a grim line, and she glared right back at him.

"You still won't leave, though, will you?"

"No. I won't. Not until you're on the mend."

"I am mending."

"Not fast enough and you know it. So suck it up and let's get the job done, all right?"

"Stubbornest damn woman I've ever known," he muttered darkly and, using his cane to take most of his weight, took the steps to the drive. The minute his feet hit the drive, both ranch dogs stopped their playing, leaped up, ears perked, then with yips of delight, charged at him.

"Oh, for heaven's sake." Maggie jumped out in front of him to keep the too-exuberant dogs from crashing into Justice and bowling him right over, but it wasn't necessary.

"Angel. Spike." Justice's voice was like

thunder, and when he snapped his fingers, both dogs instantly obeyed. As one, they skidded to a stop and dropped to the ground, their chins on their front paws as they looked up at him.

Maggie laughed in spite of herself. Going down on one knee, she petted each of the dogs in turn, then looked up at the man watching her. "I'd forgotten just how good you were at that. The dogs always did listen to you."

One corner of his mouth quirked briefly. "Too bad I could never get you to do the same."

Straightening up, Maggie met his gaze. "I never was the kind of woman to jump at the snap of your fingers, Justice. Not for you, not for anyone."

"Wouldn't have had you jump," he told her.

"Really. And what command would you have had me follow if you could?"

He shifted his gaze from hers, looked toward the barn and the pastures beyond and said softly, "Stay."

Six

A ping of regret echoed inside Maggie at his statement, sending out ripples of reaction like the energy released when a tuning fork was struck. Her entire body seemed to ache as she watched him walk away, keeping his gaze averted.

"You would have told me to stay?" she repeated, hearing the break in her own voice and hating it. "How can you say that to me now?"

He didn't answer her, just kept walking slowly, carefully. The only sign of his own emotions being engaged was how tightly he held on to his cane. Maggie's back teeth ground together. The man was just infuriating. She could tell that he was regretting what he had said, but that was just too bad for him.

The first time she'd walked away from him and their marriage, it had nearly ripped her heart out of her chest. He hadn't said a word to her. He'd watched her go, and she'd felt then that he hadn't really cared. She'd told herself through her tears that clearly their marriage hadn't been everything she'd thought it was. That the dream of family she was giving up on had been based in her own fantasies, not reality.

She'd thought that Justice couldn't possibly have loved her as much as she loved him. Not if he could let her go without a word.

Then months later, they shared that last weekend together—and created Jonas—and still, he'd let her go. He'd stayed crouched behind his walls and locked away whatever he was thinking or feeling. He'd simply shot down her dreams again and dismissed her.

And even then she hadn't been able to file the signed divorce papers when he'd returned them to her. Instead, she'd tucked them away, gone through her pregnancy, delivered their son and waited. Hoping that Justice would come to her.

Naturally, he hadn't.

"How could you do it?" she whispered and thought she saw his shoulders flinch. "How could you let me leave when you wanted me to stay? Why, Justice? You didn't say a *word* to me when I left. Either time."

He stopped dead and even the cool wind sliding in off the ocean seemed to still. The dogs went quiet and it felt as if the world had taken a breath and held it.

"What was there to say?" His jaw tightened and he bit off each word as if it tasted bitter.

"You could have asked me to stay."

"No," he said, heading once more for the barn. "I couldn't."

Maggie sighed and walked after him, measuring her steps to match his more halting ones. Of course he couldn't ask her to stay, she thought.

"Oh, no, not you. Not Justice King," she grumbled and kicked at the dirt. "Don't want anyone to know you're actually capable of feeling something."

He stopped again and this time he turned his head to look at her. "I feel plenty, Maggie," he said. "You should know that better than anyone."

"How can I know that, Justice?" She threw her hands high, then let them fall to her sides again. "You won't tell me what you're thinking. You never did. We laughed, we made love but you never let me *inside,* Justice. Not once."

Something in his dark blue eyes flashed. "You got in. You just didn't stay long enough to notice."

Had she? She couldn't be sure. In the beginning of their marriage, it was all heat and fire. They hadn't been able to keep their hands off each other. They took long rides, they spent lazy rainy days in bed and Maggie would have told anyone who had asked that she and Justice were truly happy.

But, God knew, it hadn't taken much to shake the foundations of what they'd shared, so how real could any of it have been?

Her shoulders slumped as she watched him continue on to the barn. He held himself straighter, taller, as if knowing she'd be watching and not wanting to look anything but his usual, strong self. How typical was that, Maggie thought.

Justice King never admitted weakness. He'd always been a man unable to ask for anything—not even for help if he needed it—because he would never acknowledge needing assistance in the first place. He was always so self-reliant that it was nearly a religion to him. She'd known that from the beginning of their relationship, and still she wished things had been different.

But if wishes were horses, as the old saying went…

Maggie was shaken and not too proud to admit it, at least to herself. Pushing her turbulent thoughts to a back corner of her mind to be examined later, she took a deep breath, forced some lightheartedness into her voice and quickly changed the subject.

"So," she asked, glancing back at the two dogs trotting behind them, "why are Angel and Spike here instead of out with the herd?"

There was a pause before he answered, as if he were grateful for the reprieve.

"We're training two new dogs to help out," he said. "Phil thought it best to give these two a couple days off while the new pups are put through their paces."

She'd been a rancher's wife long enough to know the value of herd dogs. When the dogs worked the cattle, they could get into tight places a cowboy and his horse couldn't. The right dog could get a herd moving and keep it moving while never scaring the cattle into a stampede, which could cause injury both to cowboys and to herd. These dogs were well trained and were spoiled rotten by the cowboys, as she remembered. She'd teased Justice once that apparently sheepherders had been right about using dogs in their work and that finally ranchers had caught on.

She smiled, remembering how Justice had reacted—chasing her through the house and up the stairs, laughing, until he'd caught up to her in their bedroom. Then he'd spent the next several hours convincing her to take it back. No cattleman alive had ever taken advice from a sheepherder, he'd told her, least of all him.

Spike and Angel darted past Justice and Maggie, heading through the open doors of a barn that was two stories tall and built to match the main house's log construction. The shadows were deep, and the only sound coming from the barn was that deep, insistent lowing Maggie had heard earlier.

"Hey, you two, come away from there!" A sudden shout came from inside the barn, and almost instantly both dogs scuttled back outside and took off in a fast lope across the dirt. If they'd been children, Maggie was sure they would have been laughing.

"What's that about?" she asked, watching the dogs race each other to the water tank kept as a sort of swimming pool for herd dogs.

"Mike's got a cow and her calf in there. Probably didn't want the dogs getting too close," Justice told her, walking through the barn to the last stall on the right. There he leaned one arm on the top of the wood partition, clearly to take some weight off his leg, and watched as an older man expertly ran his hands up and down a nearly three-month-old calf's foreleg.

"How's he doing?"

"Better," Mike said, without looking up. "Swelling's down, so he and his mama can go back out to pasture tomorrow." Then he did lift his gaze and smiled when he spotted Maggie. "Well, now, you're a sight for sore eyes. Good to see you back home, Maggie."

"Thanks, Mike." She'd gotten more of a welcome from the cowboys and hired hands than she had from her own husband, she thought wryly. "So what happened to this little guy?"

Maggie wandered into the stall, keeping one wary eye on the calf's mother, then sank to one knee beside the smaller animal. He was, like most of Justice's herd, Black Angus. His black hide was the color of the shadows filling the barn, and his big brown eyes watched her with interest.

"Not sure, really," Mike said. "One of the boys saw the little guy limping out on the range, so he brought them in. But whatever was wrong, looks like it's all right now."

The calf wasn't small anymore. He was about six months old and wearing the King Ranch brand on his flank. He was well on his way to being the size of his father, which would put him, full grown, at about eleven hundred pounds. But the way he cuddled up to his mother, looking for food and comfort, made him seem like little more than an over-large puppy.

The mingled aromas of hay and leather and cow mingled together in the vast barn and somehow made a soothing sort of scent. Maggie never would have believed she was capable of thinking that, since before meeting and marrying Justice, she had been a devout city girl. She'd once thought that there was nothing lovelier than a crowded shopping mall with a good-size latte stand. She had never liked the outdoors as a kid and had considered staying in a motel as close to camping as she ever wanted to get.

And yet being on the King Ranch had been so easy. Was it just because she'd loved Justice so much? Or was it because her heart had finally figured out where she belonged?

But then, she asked herself sadly, what did it matter now?

"See you later, Mike," she said, then tugged at Justice's arm. "Let's get you moving again. Gotta get your exercise in whether you want to or not."

"I never noticed that slave-driver mentality of yours before," Justice muttered as they left the barn and wandered around the side of the main house.

"You just didn't pay attention," she told him. "It was always there."

He was moving less easily, she noticed, and instinctively she slowed her pace. He fell into her rhythm and his steps evened out again. She knew how much he hated this. Knew that he detested having to depend on others to do things for him. And she knew he was in pain, though heaven knew he'd be roasted over live coals and still not admit to that. So she started talking, filling the silence so he would have to concentrate on something other than how hard it was to walk.

"Phil said you planted new grasses?" That was a brilliant stroke, Maggie thought. Get the man talking about the ranch and the prairie grass pastures and he'd get so involved, he wouldn't notice anything else. Not even pain.

"On the high pasture," he told her, easing around the corner of the log house to walk toward a rose garden that had originally been planted by his mother. "With the herd rotation, we'll keep the cattle off that grass until winter, and if it holds and we get some rain this fall, we'll have plenty of rich feed for the herd."

"Sounds good," she murmured, knowing her input wasn't needed.

"It was a risk, taking the cattle off that section early in the rotation, but we wanted to try out the new grasses and it had to have time to settle in and grow before winter, so…" He shrugged, looked down at her and unexpectedly smiled. "You're taking my mind off my leg, aren't you?"

"Well," she said, enjoying the full measure of a Justice King smile for as long as she could, "yeah. I am. Is it working?"

"It is," he said with a nod. "But I'm going to stop talking about it before you fall asleep while walking."

"It was interesting," she argued.

"Sure. That's why your eyes are glazed over."

Maggie sighed. "Okay, so the pastures aren't exactly thrilling conversational tidbits. But if you're talking about the ranch, you're not thinking about your leg."

He stopped, reached down and rubbed his thigh as if just the mention of it had fired up the aching muscles. He tipped his head back and looked up at the sky, a broad expanse of blue, dotted with thick white clouds. "I'm tired of thinking about my leg. Tired of the cane. Tired of being in the house when I should be on the ranch."

"Justice—"

"It's all right, Maggie," he said with a shake of his head. "I'm just impatient, that's all."

She nodded, understanding. She'd seen this before, usually in men, but some women had the same reaction. They felt as though their worlds would fall apart and crash if they weren't on top of everything at all times. Only they were capable of running their business, their homes, their children. It was a hard thing to accept help, especially since it meant also accepting that you could be replaced. However briefly.

"The garden looks good," she said abruptly.

He turned his head to look. "It does. Mom's roses are just starting to bloom."

Maggie led the way down the wide dirt path, lined on either side by pale, cream-colored bricks. The perfume of the roses was thicker the farther they went into the garden, and she inhaled deeply, dragging that scent into her lungs.

The rose garden spread out just behind the ranch house. A huge flagstone patio off the kitchen and great room led directly here, and Maggie had often had her morning coffee at the kitchen table, staring out at the garden Justice said his mother had loved.

The garden was laid out in circles, each round containing a different color and kind of rose. Justice's mother had turned this section of the ranch into a spring and summer wonder. Soon, Maggie knew, the garden would be bursting with color and scent.

She heard him behind her and turned to look at him. Behind him, the house sat, windows glistening in the sun. To her right was a stone bench, and she heard the splash of the water from the fountain that sat directly in the middle of the garden.

Justice was looking at her through narrowed eyes and, not for the first time, Maggie wondered what he was thinking about. What he saw when he looked at her. Did he have the same regrets she did? When he looked at the roses his mother had planted, did he see Maggie there, too? Was she imprinted on this house, his memories? Or had she become someone he didn't *want* to think about at all?

Well, that was depressing, she told herself and shook off the feeling deliberately. Instead, she cocked her head to one side, looked up at him and asked, "Do you remember that summer storm?"

After a second or two, he smiled and nodded. "Hard to forget that one." He glanced around at the neatly laid out flower beds, then kicked at one of the bricks at his feet. "It's the reason we laid these bricks, remember?"

A soft wind blew in and lifted her hair off her neck and Maggie grinned. "How could I forget? It rained so hard the roses were coming up out of the ground." She looked around and saw the place as it had been that long-ago night. "The ground couldn't hold any more water. And the roots of the bushes were pulling up just from the weight of the bushes themselves." She and Justice had raced outside, determined to save his mother's garden. "We were running around here for two hours, in the rain and the mud, propping up the rose bushes, trying to keep them all from being washed away."

"We did it, too," he mused, looking around now, as if reassuring himself that they'd been successful.

"Yeah, we did." She took a breath and asked, "Remember how we celebrated?"

His gaze fixed on hers, and she felt the heat of that stare slide right down into her bones. "You mean how we made love out here, covered in mud, laughing like loons?"

"Yes," she said, "that's what I mean." She took an instinctive step toward him. The past mingled with the present, memory tangling with fresh need. Her mouth went dry, her insides melted and something low and deep within her pulsed with desire. Passion. She remembered the feel of his hands on her. The taste of his mouth on hers. The heavy weight of him pressing her down, into cold, sodden earth. And she remembered she hadn't felt the cold. Hadn't noticed the rain. All she'd been aware of was Justice.

Some things didn't change.

The sun was blazing out of a spring sky. They were on opposite sides of a very large fence that snaked between them. Their marriage was supposedly over, and all that was keeping her here on the ranch was the fact that he needed her to help him be whole again.

And yet, none of that mattered.

She took another step toward him. He moved closer, too, his gaze locked on hers, heat sizzling in those dark blue depths until Maggie almost needed to fan herself. What he wanted was there on his face. As she was sure it was on hers. She needed him. Always had. Probably always would.

Standing here surrounded by memories was

just stoking those needs, magnifying them with the images from the past. She didn't care. Maggie lifted one hand, cupped his cheek in her palm and felt the scratch of beard stubble against her skin. It felt good. Right. He closed his eyes at her touch, blew out a breath and moved even closer to her.

"Maggie…"

A baby's cry broke them apart.

Jolting, Maggie turned toward the sound and saw Mrs. Carey hurrying across the patio and down the steps, carrying a very fussy Jonas on her hip. The older woman had cropped gray hair and was wearing jeans and a long-sleeved T-shirt. Her tennis shoes didn't make a sound as she scurried toward them, an apologetic expression on her face.

Maggie walked to meet the woman, holding out her arms for her son. Jonas practically flung himself at his mother and wrapped his arms around her neck.

"I'm so sorry for interrupting," Mrs. Carey

said, glancing from Maggie to Justice with a shrug. "But Jonas looked out the window, saw his mama and there was just no holding him back."

"It's okay, Mrs. Carey," Maggie told her, running one hand up and down her son's back in a soothing gesture that was already quieting the baby's cries and sniffles. The look on the housekeeper's face told Maggie she *really* regretted interrupting whatever had been going on. But maybe it was for the best, she thought. Maybe things would have gotten even more complicated if she and Justice had allowed themselves to be swept away by memories.

It only took another moment for Jonas to lift his head from Maggie's shoulder and give her a watery smile. "There now, no reason to cry, is there, little man?"

Jonas huffed out a tiny breath, grabbed hold of one of Maggie's earrings, then turned his victorious smile on Justice and Mrs. Carey. As if he were saying, *See? I have my mommy. Just like I wanted.*

Justice moved off a little and sat down hard on the stone bench. "I'm done exercising, Maggie. Why don't you take your son into the house?"

Mrs. Carey, standing behind her boss, made a face at him that almost set Maggie laughing. But the truth was she was just too torn to smile about the situation. There her stubborn husband sat, with his son within arm's reach, and Justice had withdrawn from them. Sealed himself off behind that damn wall of his. Well, Maggie thought, maybe it was past time she tore some of that wall down. Whether he liked it or not.

Giving into the urge, Maggie jostled Jonas on her hip a bit, then asked, "Jonas, you want to go see your daddy?"

Justice's head snapped up and his eyes were wide and horrified briefly before they narrowed into dangerous slits. "I'm not his daddy."

"You are the most hardheaded, stubborn,

foolish man I have ever known," Mrs. Carey muttered darkly. "Not enough sense to see the truth even when it's staring right at you with your own eyes."

"You might want to remember who you work for," Justice told her without looking at her, keeping his eyes fixed on Maggie and the boy.

"I believe I just described who I work for," Mrs. Carey told him. "Now I'm going back to the kitchen. Put a roast in for dinner."

When she was gone, Maggie stared at Justice for another minute, while the baby laughed and babbled to himself. But her mind was made up. She was going to force Justice to acknowledge their son. No more of this letting him avoid the baby, scuttling out of rooms just as she entered. No more walking a wide berth around the situation. It was time for him to be shaken up a bit. And there was no better way to do it than this.

"Here you go, sweetie. Go see your daddy." Maggie swung Jonas down and before Justice could get off the bench, she plopped the baby into his lap.

Both baby and man wore the same startled expression, and they looked so much alike that Maggie actually laughed.

Justice didn't hear her. He was holding his breath and watching the baby on his lap as if it were a live grenade. He expected the tiny boy to start shrieking in protest at being handed over to a stranger. But instead, Jonas looked up at him and a slow, cautious smile curved his tiny mouth.

He had two teeth, on the bottom, Justice noted, and a stream of drool sliding out of his mouth. His hair was black, his eyes a dark blue and his arms and legs were chubby pistons, moving at an incredible rate. Justice kept one hand on the boy's back and felt the rapid beat of the baby's heart beneath his hand.

For days he'd steered clear of the child, told himself the baby was none of his concern. He hadn't wanted to be touched by the child.

Hadn't wanted to look at Jonas and know that Maggie had found what she needed with some other man. Staying away had been much easier.

Yet now, as he considered that, he realized that for the first time in his life, he'd behaved like a coward. He'd run from the child and what he meant to save his own ass. To protect himself.

What did that say about him?

Jonas laughed and Justice turned his attention to Maggie, who was watching them both with tears in her eyes. His heart turned over in his chest, and just for an instant he let himself believe it was real. That he and Maggie were together again. That Jonas was his son.

Then the sound of a car engine out front shattered the quiet. A moment later that engine was shut off and the solid slam of a car door followed. Before he could wonder who had arrived, Mrs. Carey shouted from inside, "Jesse and Bella are here!"

Justice stared up at Maggie, the moment over. "Take the baby."

Seven

"**I** can't tell you how glad I'll be to finally have this baby," Bella said with a groan as she eased back into one of the comfy chairs in the great room. Her long, dark hair lay across her shoulder in a thick braid and silver hoops winked from her ears. A wry smile curved her mouth as she ran one hand over her belly. "It's not all about wanting to sleep on my stomach again, though. I'm just so anxious to meet whoever's in there."

"You didn't find out the baby's sex?" Mrs. Carey asked.

"No," Bella said. "We decided to be surprised."

Maggie grinned. She'd felt the same way. She hadn't wanted to know the sex of her baby before she saw him for the first time. And she remembered all too clearly what the last couple of weeks of pregnancy were like. No wonder Bella was fidgety. There was the discomfort, of course. But more than that, there was a sense of breathless expectation that clung to every moment.

"And," Bella was saying, "I don't think Jesse can take much more of this. The man's on a constant red alert. Every time I breathe too deeply, he bolts for the phone, ready to call 911. He's so nervous that he's awake every couple of hours during the night, waking me up to make sure I'm all right."

"That's just as it should be," Mrs. Carey said, from her seat on the couch, where she held Jonas in the crook of her arm and fed him his afternoon bottle. "A man should be wrapped up in the birth of his child." She sniffed. "Some men, at least, know what to do."

It was really nice having the King family housekeeper on her side, Maggie mused, but at the same time, she felt she owed Justice some sort of defense.

"To be fair," Maggie said, "Justice didn't know I was pregnant."

"Would have if he hadn't been too stubborn to go after you in the first place," she countered with a sharp nod that said, that's all there is to it. "If he had, then you would have been here, at home while you were carrying this little sweetheart. And I wouldn't have had to wait so long to meet him."

It would have been nice, Maggie thought, to have been here, surrounded by love and concern during her pregnancy. Instead, she'd lived alone, in her apartment a half hour away in Long Beach. Thank God she'd had her own family for support.

"I can't believe you went through your whole pregnancy on your own," Bella said softly, her hands still moving restlessly over the mound of her belly. "I don't know what I would have done without Jesse."

"It wasn't easy," Maggie admitted, pouring Bella another glass of lemonade before slumping back into her own chair. She shot a quick look at her baby, happily ensconced in Mrs. Carey's arms, and remembered those months of loneliness. She'd missed Justice so much then and had nearly called him dozens of times. But her own pride had discounted that notion every time it presented itself. "I had my family," she said, reminding herself that she'd never really been completely alone. Besides, she didn't want these women feeling sorry for her. She hadn't had Justice with her, but she hadn't been miserable the whole time, either.

"That's good," Bella said softly, as if she understood exactly what Maggie was trying to do.

"My parents live in Arizona, but they were on the phone all the time and were really supportive. Both of my sisters were fabulous." Maggie grinned suddenly with a memory. "My sister Mary Theresa was even in the delivery room with me. Matrice was great, really. Don't know what I would have done without her there."

"I'm glad you weren't alone," Mrs. Carey said quietly, "but a woman should have her man at her side when her children are born."

In a perfect world, Maggie thought but didn't say. Instead, she sighed and said, "I wanted to tell him. I really did. But at the same time, Justice had already told me that he didn't want children."

Mrs. Carey snorted. "Darn fool. Don't know why he'd say that raised in this family, one of four kids. Why wouldn't he want children?

Especially," she added, bending to kiss Jonas's forehead, "this little darling."

Maggie gave her a smile, delighted that Jonas had an honorary grandmother to dote on him. "I didn't understand why, either, but he'd made himself clear. So I couldn't very well show up here pregnant knowing how he felt about it. And besides…"

"You wanted him to want you for *you,* not for the baby," Bella said for her.

"Exactly," Maggie said on another sigh. She may have just met Bella King, but she had a feeling the two of them could be very close friends. But that wasn't likely to happen either, since the minute Justice recovered, she'd be leaving again—and this time she knew it would be for good. There'd be no coming back here, not if Justice could turn his back on his son.

With a heavy heart, Maggie glanced around the room and idly noted the splash of sunshine lying across polished floors and gleaming tables. The scent of freshly cut flowers hung in the air, and the only sounds were those made by her hungry son as he devoted himself to his snack.

"I understand that completely," Bella told her. "If I'd been in your situation, I would have done the same thing. You know, Jesse told me how happy you and his brother were together. And I can tell you he was really surprised when you two split up."

Mrs. Carey huffed out a disgusted breath.

"He wasn't the only one." Maggie felt a quick sting of tears behind her eyes, and she blinked fiercely to keep them at bay. The time for tears was long past. "I would never have believed that Justice and I wouldn't be together forever. But he's just so darn…"

"Stubborn. Bullheaded," Mrs. Carey supplied.

"That about covers it," Maggie said with a laugh, relieved to feel her emotions settle again.

"So is Jesse," Bella said, then went on to describe life with a husband who rarely let her walk across the room without an escort. She started in by telling them how her office at King Beach had been outfitted with a resting chaise and that Jesse made sure she took a nap every afternoon.

While Maggie listened, she tried to hide the pain she felt. The envy, wrapping itself around her heart, for what Bella shared with her husband. Jesse had already come into the room twice in the past hour, ordering his wife to put her feet up, getting her a pillow for her aching back.

It was easy to imagine that Bella's whole pregnancy had been like that. With her eager, loving husband dancing attendance on her. And Maggie couldn't help but remember what her own pregnancy had been like. Sure, she'd had her parents and her sisters, but she hadn't had Justice. She hadn't had the luxury of lying in bed beside the father of her child while they spun daydreams about their baby's future. She hadn't been able to share the excitement of a new ultrasound photo. Hadn't been able to hold Justice's hand to her belly so that he could feel Jonas moving around inside her.

They'd both missed so much. Maybe she should have come to Justice immediately on finding out she was pregnant. Maybe she should have given him the chance then to acknowledge their child, to let them both into his life. But she'd been so sure she wouldn't be welcome. And frankly, his actions over the past few days supported her decision.

But then she remembered the look in Justice's eyes just an hour or so ago when she'd dropped Jonas into his lap. There had been an unexpected tenderness on his face, underlying the surprise and wariness. Maybe, she thought wistfully, if she'd just stood her ground long ago, things might have been different. Now, though, she'd never know for sure.

"You all right, honey?"

Mrs. Carey's concerned voice brought Maggie out of her thoughts to focus on what was happening. She shot a look at Bella in time to see a quick flash of pain dart over her features. "Bella?"

"I'm okay," she said, taking a deep breath. "It's just that my back's been bothering me all day. Probably just spasms from carrying around all this extra weight."

"A backache?" Maggie asked.

"All day?" Mrs. Carey added.

Bella grimaced, then said, "I probably just need another cookie."

"Um," Maggie started, "just when exactly are you due, Bella?"

"Oh, not for two weeks yet." She groaned a little as she pushed herself forward to reach for the plate on the table in front of her.

Maggie and Mrs. Carey exchanged a long, knowing look.

"You're crazy, you know that, right?" Jesse took a long pull of his beer and stretched his legs out in front of him, crossing them at the ankle.

Justice shot a look at his younger brother in time to see him shaking his head in disgust. The sun was hot, the breeze was cool and the patio was empty except for him and Jesse.

Maggie, Bella and Mrs. Carey were all in the house cooing over Jonas and talking about Bella's due-any-minute baby. He scowled to himself and took a drink of his own beer. Justice and Maggie had already legally separated by the time Bella and Jesse got together, but you wouldn't have known it from the way Maggie and Bella had instantly bonded. They were like two old friends already, and their chatter had eventually chased Jesse and Justice out to the patio for some quiet.

At least, that had been the plan.

"Crazy? Me?" Justice laughed shortly. "I'm not the one hauling my extremely pregnant wife around when she should be at home."

"Bella gets antsy sitting around the house. Besides, we're only forty minutes from the hospital—and you're changing the subject."

"Damn straight. Take the hint."

Jesse grinned, completely unfazed by Justice's snarl. "Why should I?"

"Because it's none of your business."

"When's that ever stopped a King?"

True, Justice thought. Never had a King been born who knew enough to keep his nose out of his brother's business.

"Look," Jesse said, "Jeff called, told me he'd hired Maggie, so I thought I'd bring Bella over to meet her sister-in-law. Nobody told me you had a son."

"I don't."

Laughing shortly, Jesse said, "You're so busy being a tight ass you don't even see it, do you?"

"I'm not talking about this with you, Jesse."

"Fine. Then I'll talk. You listen."

A cloud scudded across the sun, tossing the patio into shadow and dropping the temperature suddenly. Justice frowned at his brother, but Jesse paid no attention. He sat up, braced his forearms on his thighs and held his beer bottle between his palms. "I thought your leg was hurt, not your eyes."

"What's that supposed to mean?"

"It means, you dumb jerk, that Jonas looks just like you and you'd have to be blind not to see it."

"Black hair and blue eyes doesn't make him mine."

"It's more than that and you know it. The shape of his face. His nose. His hands. Damn it, Justice, he's a carbon copy of you."

"He can't be."

"Why the hell not?" Jesse's voice dropped and his gaze narrowed. "Why can't he be your son?"

Irritated beyond measure, pushed beyond endurance, Justice awkwardly got out of his chair and grabbed for his hated cane. Then he walked a few uneasy steps away from Jesse, stared out at the rose garden and told his brother what he'd never told another living soul before.

"Because I can't have kids."

"Says who?"

Justice choked out a laugh. Figured Jesse wouldn't react with any kind of tact. Just accept what his brother said and let it go. "A doctor. Right after the accident that killed Mom and Dad and laid me up for weeks."

"You never said anything."

He laughed again, a sound that was harsh and miserable even to his own ears. "Would you have?"

"No," Jesse said, standing up to walk to his side. "I guess not. But, Justice, doctors make mistakes."

He took a drink of his beer, letting the frothy cold liquid coat his insides and put out the fires of humiliation and regret burning within. "Not about that."

"God, you're an idiot."

"I'm getting awful tired of people calling me names," Justice muttered.

"You deserve it. How do you know that

doctor wasn't wrong?" Jesse stepped out in front of him, forcing Justice to meet his gaze. "Did you ever get a second opinion?"

"You think I *liked* getting that news? Why would I go to someone else to hear the same damn thing again?"

Shaking his head wildly as if he couldn't believe what he'd just heard, Jesse blinked at his brother and said, "I don't know, to make sure the guy was right? Justice, you get a second opinion from vets on your cattle! Why wouldn't you do that for yourself?"

Justice wiped one hand across his face, then took another long swallow of his beer. He didn't like defending himself and liked even less the vague notion that his younger brother might be right. What if that doctor *had* been wrong? What if it had all been a mistake?

His heartbeat thundered in his chest and his mouth went dry. If that were true, then he'd let Maggie walk out of his life for no reason at all. And worse, he had a son he'd only just met.

"No, he wasn't wrong," Justice muttered, refusing to accept the possibility. "He couldn't have been."

"Why?" Jesse demanded. "Because if he was wrong, that means you've wasted time with Maggie, neglected your son and are the Grand Poobah of Idiots?"

Grinding his back teeth together, Justice barely managed to mutter, "Pretty much."

"Well, here's something else for you to think about, your majesty. Even if he was right at the time, things change. But you never bothered to find out, did you? Damn, Justice. You really are—"

"—an idiot. Yeah, I know. Thanks for not saying it again."

"Give me time," Jesse told him with a half grin. "I'll get around to it."

"I'm sure. Y'know, I just told Jeff that I should have been born an only child."

"Like you could have made it through life without us!" Jesse laughed and clapped

Justice on the shoulder. "Now, you know what you've got to do, right?"

"I have a feeling you're about to tell me."

"As you like to say, damn straight. Get a paternity test, Justice. It's easy. It's fast. And it'll tell you flat out if the doctor was wrong or not."

Paternity test. It would be easier, he thought, than finding another doctor and going through testing again himself. And he'd have his answer. One way or the other. A thread of worry snaked its way through his system, reminding him that if the results came back as negative, then he'd have to acknowledge that Maggie had lied to him. And that she had another man in her life. He ignored that worry completely.

"Maybe you're right," he murmured.

Jesse laughed. "Hell, it was worth the drive to the ranch just to hear you say that."

"Funny. That's really funny."

"This isn't." Jesse's smile faded and his voice dropped a notch. "Get this straightened out,

Justice. Because if you don't, you're going to lose Maggie, your son, everything. Then you'll be a miserable bastard for the rest of your life and speaking as one of the people who'd have to put up with it, we'd rather not see that."

"You made your point." Justice had had more advice from people in the past couple of weeks than he'd had in the past five years. And he was damn tired of it.

"Glad to hear it. Now, how about another beer?"

"What the hell—"

"*Justice!*"

Maggie's shout had him spinning around and nearly toppling over but for Jesse's hand on his arm steadying him. She stood in the open doorway leading to the kitchen, and the wind swept her fiery hair into a dancing tangle around her head. "What is it?"

"It's Bella," Maggie called back, her gaze sliding from Justice to Jesse, who was already sprinting for the house. "It's time."

* * *

"How much longer?"

Maggie looked up at Justice and smiled. They'd been at the hospital for nearly five hours already and it felt like days. Funny, but when she herself had been in labor, it had seemed that time was rushing by, breathlessly. Now that she was expected to do nothing but sit and wait, time was at a crawl.

"No way to tell," she told him, tossing aside a six-month-old magazine she hadn't been reading anyway. "First-time babies can take anywhere from a few hours to a couple of days to make their appearance."

Justice looked horrified and Maggie stifled a laugh. He'd been a nervous wreck since they first bundled Jesse and Bella into the ranch SUV and hit the freeway. Neither of them had trusted Jesse to drive. He'd been practically vibrating with nerves when he called Bella's doctor to tell her they were headed to the hospital. Leaving Jonas with Mrs. Carey,

Maggie had ridden shotgun while Justice drove and Jesse hovered over Bella on the backseat.

As soon as they had arrived at the sprawling medical center in Irvine, Jesse and Bella had been taken off to Maternity. Justice and Maggie, meanwhile, had been directed to the waiting room, which boasted the most uncomfortable chairs in the world. Short backs, narrow seats and hardwood arms made getting comfy a nearly impossible feat.

But, she supposed, comfort wasn't a real issue, since mostly the people waiting for news from the delivery room were too nervous to sit anyway. Still, she kept giving it a shot. "Justice, sit down and give your leg a rest, why don't you?"

"My leg's fine," he said, but his tight-lipped expression told the real truth. She knew he was in pain, but the man would never admit it.

"Okay, then sit down because you're making me nervous," she said.

He looked at her for a long minute, then

took a seat beside her. A television was tuned to a twenty-four-hour comedy channel, the canned laughter and muttered conversations becoming a sort of white noise in the background. The walls were a pale hospital green and the carpet was multicolored, probably in an attempt to keep it from showing wear over the years. The scent of burned coffee hung in the air, a nasty layer over the medicinal stench of antiseptic.

"I hate waiting," Justice muttered, throwing a glance at the door opening onto the hallway that led to Labor and Delivery.

"No kidding? You hide it well." Maggie patted his arm absentmindedly.

Two other people, an older couple, were waiting in that room with them, having arrived just a half hour ago. The woman leaned forward and excitedly confided, "My daughter's about to make me a grandmother. It's a boy. His name will be Charlie, after my husband."

"Congratulations," Maggie said. "We're waiting to become an aunt and uncle."

"Isn't it wonderful?" The woman was practically glowing as she reached out blindly and took her husband's hand. "So thrilling to be a part of a miracle. Even in a small way."

Beside her, Justice shifted in his chair, but Maggie ignored him. "You're right, it is."

"The waiting is difficult, though," the woman admitted. "I'd do much better if I only knew what was happening…."

Whatever the woman might have said next was lost forever when a nurse in surgical scrubs poked her head in the door, smiling and asked, "Mr. and Mrs. Baker?"

"Yes!" The expectant grandmother leaped up out of her chair and would have rushed blindly at the nurse if her husband hadn't dropped both hands onto her shoulders. "That's us. How is Alison? Our daughter?"

"She's doing great and said to tell you that Charlie is calling for you."

"Ohmygoodness!" The woman turned her face into her husband's chest and, after a quick hug, looked back at the nurse. "We can see them now?"

"Of course. Follow me."

"What about us?" Justice demanded.

The nurse turned a questioning look on him. "I'm sorry?"

"It's nothing," Maggie told her, taking Justice's hand and giving it a squeeze. "Never mind."

"Good luck to you, dear," the new grandma said as they hustled out of the room after the nurse.

"What do you mean it's nothing?" Justice asked when they were gone. "We were here long before them!"

Maggie laughed at her husband's impatience. "Not exactly how it works, Justice."

"Well, it damn well should." He pushed up and out of his chair again, marched to the door and looked out. Then he turned back to her and said, "I feel like the walls are closing in on me in here. I don't think I can stay in this little room another minute."

"I'm kind of with you on that," Maggie said. "Let's take a walk."

For the next several hours, Justice and Maggie prowled the hallways of the hospital, checking in occasionally with the maternity ward. They wandered down to the nursery to look at the new babies and once again ran into the Bakers, who proudly pointed out little Charlie. They checked in with the nurses' station to get updates on Bella, and Maggie called the ranch to be assured by Mrs. Carey that Jonas had had his supper and his bath and was now sleeping soundly. She was told not to worry and to be sure to call the minute the baby was born.

"How did you do it?" Justice asked quietly when they were once more in the dreaded waiting room.

"Hmm? Do what?"

"This," he said, waving a hand as if to encompass the hospital, the maternity ward and all they contained. "How did you do it alone?"

"I wasn't alone," she told him. "Matrice was with me."

"Your sister." He blew out a breath. "You should have told me. I would have been here."

Outside, night crouched at the windows. The lights in the waiting room were dim, and thankfully, they had shut off the television, since they were the only two people in the room. Now she almost wished for that background noise so that the silence between them wouldn't seem so overwhelming.

Looking into Justice's eyes now, she would have liked to believe he was right. That had she called him from the hospital, he would have rushed right over to be at her side. But she knew better. In her heart of hearts, she just knew.

"No, you wouldn't have, Justice," she said with a sigh. "You wouldn't have believed me then any more than you do now."

He pushed one hand through his long black hair, scrubbed the other across the back of his neck and admitted, "Maybe you're right. Maybe I wouldn't have believed you. But I would have come to you anyway, Maggie. I would have been with you through this."

Something inside her eased just a little. To know that—to believe that he would have come whether or not he thought he was her baby's father was a gift. Yet even as she admitted that, there was another voice inside her demanding to be heard.

"Do you really think I would have wanted you here if you thought I was lying to you?" Before he could answer, she added, "And do you really believe that I would have called you to watch me give birth to another man's child?"

He watched her as long silent moments ticked past. Finally, though, he said, "No. You wouldn't have. To both questions." He rubbed absentmindedly at his thigh. "You really threw me hard, Maggie. Showing up at the ranch the way you did. With a boy you claim to be mine."

God, she was tired of defending herself. Sighing, she said, "He is yours. I'm not just claiming it."

He studied Maggie, his gaze moving over her features until she shifted uneasily under his steady regard. Eventually, he spoke. "I have something to tell you."

"What?" Maggie held her breath as hope jumped up inside her and waved its arms and legs excitedly. Was he finally going to admit that he knew Jonas was his? That she wasn't lying? Was he going to ask her to stay with him? Be a family?

"Mr. and Mrs. King?"

Maggie groaned at the interruption and turned her head to look at the nurse stationed in the doorway. Hours ago, she would have welcomed the woman. Now? What terrible timing. But the nurse was smiling and Maggie was already standing up to join Justice when she said, "Yes, that's us. Are Bella and the baby all right?"

"Everyone's fine," the nurse assured them. "Even the happy father is coming around."

"Coming around?" Justice repeated. "What—"

"He got a little light-headed in the delivery room," the nurse hedged.

"You mean he *fainted?*" Justice asked her, grinning like a big brother who would now have something on his sibling for the rest of his life.

"Justice…" Maggie said.

"You've been invited in to meet the newest member of your family," the nurse told them. "If you'll follow me."

"What was it?" Maggie asked. "Girl or boy?"

"I'll let the new mom tell you that," she said, leading them through a set of double doors and down a brightly lit hallway.

Two immensely pregnant women were wandering the halls, shuffling with slow steps as they hung on to IV poles for support. Their husbands were right on their heels, murmuring encouragement. In one room a woman moaned, and from yet another a new baby's indignant wail rose up like a discordant symphony.

Maggie felt Justice's hand on the small of her back and relished that small intimacy. Here at least, they were together. A team. Two people who had survived hours of expectation and were now about to be rewarded.

In Bella's room the new mom lay back, exhausted and gorgeous against her pillows, a tightly wrapped bundle cradled in her arms. Jesse stood beside her, still looking a little pale and glassy-eyed but happier than they'd ever seen him.

Maggie hurried forward, held on to the bedrail, stared down into a red, wrinkly face and declared it, "Beautiful. Just beautiful, Bella. So…boy or girl?"

"Boy," Jesse said proudly. "And we're keeping the J-name thing going, too. Uncle Justice, Aunt Maggie, I want you to meet Joshua."

Justice moved in closer, leaning over Maggie to get a good look at the newest King. She felt his breath on her cheek as he reached over, pulled the tightly wrapped white blanket down a bit so he could get a better view of the baby. She felt his indrawn breath as he studied his brother's son and heard the soft sigh escape him as he looked at Bella.

"He's a beauty, Bella. Good thing he looks like you."

"Hey!" Jesse grinned.

"Don't you think you'd better sit down?" Justice asked, a teasing note in his voice. "I hear the delivery was a little rough on you."

Jesse scowled and cast a disgusted glance at the open door even as Bella laughed delightedly. "Big-mouth nurse," he muttered before turning a look back on Justice. He jerked his head to one side, silently telling his brother he wanted to talk in private.

When they were far enough from the two women in the room, Jesse said, "I'm a father now, too, Justice. And I'm telling you, Jonas is your son. Don't lose this. Don't blow everything for your pride."

Justice, though, turned to look at Bella and Maggie, illuminated by the overhead light, both women looking down on that tiny boy with delirious smiles. "Now's not the time, Jesse."

"There's no better time, Justice," his brother told him. "Don't waste another minute."

Jesse moved back to his wife then, and Maggie soon joined Justice to go back to the ranch, leaving the new family to settle in together. As they stepped out of the hospital into the cold, clear night, Justice stopped, took a deep breath and thought about what Jesse had said to him, both here and at the ranch. What if he was right about all of it? What if Justice had been clinging to bad information for ten years?

"Wasn't he beautiful," Maggie asked, hunching deeper into the sweater she'd brought along with her. "So tiny. So perfect. So…" She stopped talking then, looked up at Justice and asked, "What is it? Is something wrong?"

He met her gaze and knew what he had to do. For all their sakes, it was time for the truth to come out.

"I want a paternity test run on Jonas."

Eight

A few days later, Justice was still feeling the effects of Maggie's fury. After an hour of lunges, wall squats and some fast walking on a treadmill, Maggie still wasn't finished with him.

She'd set up a massage table in the pool house behind the main house and had him stretched out atop it like a prisoner on a rack. Sunlight drifted in through heavily tinted windows that allowed the people inside to enjoy the view but kept anyone outside from peering in. The bubbling of the hot tub at one end of the pool sounded overly loud in the strained quiet, and quiet purr of the air conditioner sounded like a continuous sigh.

Justice paid no attention to his surroundings, though. Instead, he kept a wary eye on Maggie. Her hands were sure, her professional demeanor was firmly in place but her eyes were flashing with suppressed rage. He winced as she took hold of his foot and, lifting it, pushed his leg toward his chest. Muscles he'd been working hard stretched and pulled, and he ground his teeth together to keep any moans from sliding out of his throat.

He curled his hands around the edges of the table and held on while she forced him to push against her hands. Resistance training, she called it. Torture was more like it, Justice thought.

"You're enjoying this," he muttered.

"No, I'm not."

"Bullshit. You're pissed off and you're getting a charge out of making me pay."

"Justice," she said on a rush of breath, "I'm a professional physical therapist. I would never, under any circumstances, harm a patient under my care. Now push against me."

He did and still managed to say, "You're not trying to hurt me—I get that. But if it's a by-product, it won't bother you much, I'm thinking."

"I'm doing what's best for your rehabilitation," she said, "and resisting torturing you, despite how tempting the idea might be."

He pushed into her grip, focusing his strength, and he had to admit that since she'd been manhandling him, his leg was stronger and getting better every day. It still ached, but it was manageable and he rarely needed the cane anymore.

"I didn't ask for the test specifically to piss you off," he muttered, unwilling to leave it alone. Wanting her to see his side.

She inhaled sharply, set his leg down on the table and fisted her hands at her hips. "What do you want me to say, Justice? That I'm fine with you arranging for our son to be poked with a needle because you don't trust me? Not gonna happen."

She'd argued with him, of course, that night at the hospital. Her temper had flared and shone like a beacon as she faced him down and told him just what she thought of a man who would put an infant through an unnecessary test. But Justice hadn't been swayed.

The day he'd found out he couldn't father children, the news had almost killed him. Not only had he lost his parents—his past—in that accident, he'd lost his future as well. He was no different than any other man. He'd dreamed of family, of passing on King Ranch to another generation who would love and care for it as he had. And to have those dreams shattered in an instant had been devastating.

Yet now that Jesse had planted all of those thoughts in his mind, he had to wonder: had the doctor been wrong? He had to know the truth. Had to know if Jonas was his. If he really did have a son. And nothing Maggie said had changed his mind.

They'd arranged for the paternity test the next morning, taking the baby to one of the King laboratories. Sometimes, he told himself, it paid to be a member of a huge, successful family. The Kings had their fingers in just about every pie worth having in California. No matter what one of them might need, there was generally a cousin who could provide it.

They'd put a rush on the paternity test, and even with that it would be another few days before they had the results. Justice had never been good at waiting, and this time it was even harder. There was so much riding on the outcome of this test. Not just his pride, he told himself, but the direction of his very future.

She poured some liquid into her hands, scrubbed her palms together, then began what she called "deep tissue mobilization." In other words, a hard massage, he thought and sighed as her fingers and palms worked magic on his leg. His surgical scar was white and fresh-looking despite being completely healed. Her hands on his leg felt like a blessing. Her touch was sure, firm and, just as she said, professional. He wanted more. He wanted her hands on other parts of him, too. But he wasn't going to get that, not when she was this furious.

"How does this feel?" she asked, working from the sole of his foot, up his calf to his thigh and back down again.

If she glanced at the erection pushing at the fly of his shorts, she'd know just how it felt, he thought and grimly tried to bring his body under control. "Good," he said bluntly. "It's all good."

"You're improving, Justice. I'm glad to see it."

"Are you?"

"Of course I am. That's why I'm here, remember? And the sooner you're back on your own feet, the sooner I can take Jonas and leave."

He reached out, grabbed one of her hands

and held on. "You're not going anywhere until those test results come back in, Maggie."

She pulled her hand free of his grip. "I'm not going anywhere until my job is done," she corrected. "When it is, you won't be able to stop me from leaving."

He ran one hand over his face. "Damn it, Maggie, don't you see why I had to do this?"

"No. I don't see." She grabbed up a towel, dried her hands and continued, "You had my word, Justice. You could have believed me."

"I don't just want your word. I want proof." He pushed up onto his elbows and stared at Maggie.

Her hair was in a thick ponytail at the back of her neck. She wasn't wearing makeup, but then, she didn't really need any. Her eyes were hot and filled with fury, and her delectable mouth kept working as if she were biting back hundreds of words she wanted to fling at him.

The day was warm and she wore jeans shorts and a sleeveless T-shirt for their exercise session. Her skin was smooth and pale, and Justice wanted nothing more than to grab her, pull her down on top of him and bury himself inside her. With that mental image firmly planted in his mind, he could almost *feel* her damp heat surrounding him. Feel her body moving on his. See her as she leaned over him, brushing his chest with her bare breasts.

Damn it.

He swung his legs off the table in a hurry, hoping she hadn't seen his erection, hard and all too eager for her. Around Maggie, he seemed to be little better than a teenager. Always hard. Always ready.

"Come on," she said, stepping around the table to wrap one arm around his waist. "You need to sit in the hot tub awhile. Ease your muscles."

He thought about refusing her offer to help him walk to the far end of the pool. Then he told himself he'd be a fool for not taking the opportunity to touch her. Her scent rose up to greet him, and the soft fall of her hair against his skin felt like silk. He draped one arm across her shoulders and, with her aid, walked barefoot across the cool, sky-blue tiles lining the edge of the pool.

"Here you go," she said as they reached the partitioned-off area of the pool. There was a bench along the half circle of the hot tub, and Justice lowered himself onto it, hissing a little as the warm, bubbling water caressed his body.

"I turned the heat down a bit," Maggie was saying. "I don't want you parboiled, just warm and relaxed."

He doubted he'd ever be fully relaxed when she was around, but he didn't bother telling her that. Instead, he just looked up at her, standing on the tiles, watching him with her "professional mien" in place. Where was *his* Maggie? The one with fire in her eye. The one who turned him inside out with a single touch.

"Why don't you join me?" he asked. She started to refuse but he kept talking. "You look like you need to relax as much as I do, Maggie."

She bit her lip, blew out a breath and said, "I'm too mad at you, Justice. There wouldn't be any relaxing. For either of us."

"Fine, then," he said, slapping the frothing water with the flat of his hand. "Sit down and yell at me. You always did feel better after a good rant."

Her lips twitched and he knew he'd won.

"I don't have a bathing suit."

"I won't tell if you don't," he coaxed, mouth dry, wanting—no, *needing* to see her strip down to nothing to join him in the warm, bubbling water.

She took a deep breath and blew it out again. "Okay. But just for a few minutes. Then I should go in and take care of Jonas."

"He's fine with Mrs. Carey."

"I know that," she countered, stepping out of her jean shorts to reveal pale pink silk panties, "but he's *my* son and my responsibility."

Justice just nodded. He didn't trust himself to speak anyway. She lifted the hem of her shirt and tugged it up and over her head, giving him his first look at a wisp of a pale pink bra that exactly matched her panties. Maggie always had loved good lingerie. And he'd always considered himself a lucky bastard.

When she stepped into the water, though, he stopped her. "Aren't you going to take those off?"

She glanced down at herself, then at him. Laughing, she told him, "I don't think so. It's not safe to be naked around you, Justice."

Since his erection was now pushing against the button fly of his own shorts, demanding to be set free, he had to silently agree with her.

She eased down onto the bench opposite him and with a sigh, tipped her head back onto the rim of the pool. "God, you were right. This feels amazing."

Her lean, toned legs half floated in the water, directly in front of one of the jets, and Justice's mouth watered as he watched her. He reached down and readjusted himself, hoping to ease his discomfort. It didn't help. But he knew what would. Deftly, he undid the buttons on his shorts and pushed them off, shoving them to the floor of the pool. Instantly, his aching groin was eased, free of the constricting shorts. But he needed more.

He needed *Maggie*.

He moved closer to her while her eyes were closed. His gaze locked on her breasts, bobbing just above the water's edge, her dark, rosy nipples perfectly defined by the wet silk. She might have thought she was protecting herself by staying semiclothed, but all she'd managed to do was tempt even more thoroughly. Wet silk clung to her skin, displaying far more than it hid.

When he was close enough, he reached out to slide one hand up her calf. Instantly, her eyes flew open and she floundered a bit, until she was again seated on the bench, gaze fixed on him. "What're you doing?"

Justice moved closer still. "Helping us both relax."

"I don't think so," she said, shaking her head and scooting farther from him.

"Don't be so skittish, Maggie," he soothed. "It's not like we're strangers."

She held up one finger, holding him at bay. "No, we're not strangers, Justice. That's why we shouldn't do this. It'll only confuse things even more than they already are."

"Impossible," he countered, coming closer. The warm water felt great on his skin, the slide of his hand along her wet leg, once he took hold of her again, felt even better.

"Okay, maybe you have a point," she said, nodding. "But I'm still mad at you."

He grinned briefly. "Some of our best sex happened when you were mad at me."

"Okay," she admitted with a quick nod, "that's true, too. But that doesn't mean I want you now."

"Liar." He took hold of her foot and pulled her toward him, sliding his hands up her legs as she floated to him in the frothing water.

She hissed in a breath. "You're cheating."

"Damn straight."

"Justice, this won't solve anything."

"Maybe it doesn't have to," he told her, his hands now gripping her bottom. "Maybe it just has to happen."

She looked at him and squirmed in his grip, as if she were trying to get comfortable. "Maybe," she acknowledged. "But maybe we shouldn't let it."

"Too late," he whispered and moved off the bench so that he could turn her in his grasp, holding her floating body in front of the pulsing jets of water streaming into the tub.

"Cheating again!" she accused on a sigh as her legs parted and the thrum of the warm, pulsing water caressed her center.

While the hot tub worked its magic, Justice worked some of his own. Supporting her head with one arm, he used his free hand to undo the front clasp of her bra, freeing her breasts, her hard nipples. He dipped his head and took first one, then the other, into his mouth, rolling his tongue across their sensitive tips, feeling Maggie shudder beneath him as tumultuous sensations gathered within her.

He couldn't seem to taste her enough. How had he lived these long months without her in his arms? He suckled her, and she whimpered, both from his attentions and the steady beat of the water on her tender flesh. He knew what she was feeling because he felt it, too.

The hunger. The need. The raw urgency racing through his bloodstream. He had to have her. Reaching down, he tore her panties down and off her legs and then held her thighs apart so that the warm water could caress her even more intimately.

She grabbed at his shoulders and groaned from deep in her throat as she lifted her hips into the water jet, aching, needing. He watched her face as her eyes swam with desire and her breath caught in her throat. Then she turned her gaze on him and whispered, "I want you inside me, Justice."

That was all he needed to hear. He pulled her toward him, locked his mouth onto hers and eased them both down onto the bench. She straddled him, her knees at either side of his hips, and then lowered herself down onto him, inch by slow, incredible inch. She took him inside, into the heat. Into the heart of her, and Justice couldn't look away from her amazing eyes while he filled her, pushing himself deeply into her body.

Their gazes fixed on each other, they moved as one, racing toward the inevitable finish that they both so desperately needed. Justice felt whole. Felt complete. Felt as if nothing else in the world mattered but this moment. This woman. She was all. She was everything. And when her lips parted and she cried out his name as her body trembled and shook with the force of her release, he knew he'd never seen anything more lovely.

Only moments later, he gave himself up to the wildness calling him and willingly followed her into a dazzling world that only lovers knew.

"It didn't change anything," Maggie muttered while she dressed Jonas in his pajamas that night. Her son smiled and laughed, a rolling, full-throated sound that never failed to tear at her heart.

She had him lying on her bed, since the two of them were still sharing a room. Thank heaven it was at the opposite end of the hall from the master bedroom. After what had happened between them that afternoon, she didn't think it would be a wise idea to be too close to him.

"You think it's funny, do you?" she asked her son, smiling at him as she bent to plant a kiss on his belly. "You think Mommy is making a fool of herself? You're right, she probably is. And you know what? She's still not sorry."

The baby pulled at her hair, and Maggie gently untangled his fingers. She put first one chubby foot then the next into his footed blue sleeper, then swiftly did up the zipper, snapping the jammies closed at the neck. Jonas kicked and squirmed on Maggie's bed until she scooped him up and cuddled him close.

Nothing in the world smelled better than a baby fresh from his bath. His skin was soft and warm and the heavy, solid weight of her son in her arms eased the ache in her heart substantially.

She didn't regret making love with Justice that afternoon, but at the same time she could admit that it had probably been a mistake. Nothing was settled between them. She was still furious with him for insisting on a paternity test when any fool could look at Jonas and know without a doubt he was Justice's son. And she was frustrated by the fact that no matter how hard she tried to get past the barriers

Justice had erected around his own heart, they still stood tall and strong against her.

"But you know what really gets to me, sweetie?" she crooned, keeping her voice light and soothing as she bounced her son on her knee. "Your daddy wants a paternity test yet he's still avoiding you. Why's that, hmm? Do you know? Can you tell Mommy?"

Jonas laughed and cooed and waved his arms as if he were trying to fly, and Maggie smiled at the tiny boy who had so filled her heart. She couldn't imagine her life without Jonas now. He was a part of her. Yet, the man who was his father was still a stranger to him.

"Well, little man," she said, making her decision in an instant, "it's time we changed all that, don't you think? It's time your daddy discovered just what he's been missing. I want him to know you. To know what we could all have had together."

Jonas burbled something that Maggie took to be agreement. Pushing off the bed, she carried the baby out of the room, along the hall and down the stairs, following the sound of the evening news on a television.

She spotted Justice the moment she walked into the great room. He was sprawled in one of the comfortable chairs positioned around the room, his gaze fixed on a flat-screen TV on the opposite wall. While a news anchor rambled on about the top stories of the day, Maggie crossed the room with determined steps.

When she got close, he looked up, directly into her eyes. She felt a quick thrilling rush through her system as heat pooled in the pit of her stomach and then slipped lower. Oh, he was dangerous, she told herself, with his dark eyes, long black hair and stern features. Then his gaze shifted to the baby and a wariness shone in his eyes briefly. Which told Maggie she was doing exactly the right thing. So she took a breath, steadied herself and forced a smile.

"I brought your son to say good-night."

He sat up straighter, narrowed his gaze on her and said, "Not necessary."

"Oh, it is, Justice," she told him, and in a sure, swift movement set the baby onto Justice's lap. The two of them blinked at each other, and Maggie would have been hard-pressed to say which of them looked more surprised by her actions.

"Maggie, the test isn't in yet, so—"

"He's your son, Justice. The test will prove that, even to you, very soon. So you might as well start getting to know him."

"I don't think—"

"You should know him, Justice," she said, not letting him finish. "And there's no time like now. So, you two be good and I'll go get his bottle."

Justice's eyes widened in horror. "You're leaving me alone with him?"

Maggie laughed. "Welcome to fatherhood."

She left the room after that but stayed in the hall, peeking into the room so she could watch the two men in her life interact. Justice looked as though he were holding a ticking time bomb and Jonas looked uncertain about the whole situation.

When the baby's lower lip began to tremble, Maggie almost went back inside. Then she heard Justice say, "Now don't cry, Jonas. Everything's going to be all right."

And in the hall, Maggie had to wonder if he'd just lied to his son for the first time.

As the days passed, Justice felt the strength in his leg continue to grow. But as his body healed, his heart was being torn open. Being with Maggie and yet separate from her was harder than he would ever have thought possible. Those few stolen moments in the hot tub hadn't been repeated, and now that time with her seemed almost like a dream. A dream that continued to haunt him no matter where he was or what he was doing.

He stood at the paddock in the bright sunshine

and leaned his forearms atop the uppermost rail in the fence. With his hat pulled low over his eyes, Justice stared out at the horses being saddle-trained and told himself that he'd do well to simply concentrate on work.

Now that he was getting around better, he'd begun to take up more of the reins of the operation again, and it was good to feel more himself. Though he wasn't up yet for taking his own horse out onto the range, he would be soon. Until then, he spent as little time as possible inside the house—though he was seeing more of the baby these days. It seemed as though both Maggie and Mrs. Carey were bound and determined to see him connect with the child.

And to be honest, Justice was enjoying himself. That little boy had a way of tugging at a man's heart. Father or not, he was being drawn deeper into the web of feeling, caring. Only that morning, Jonas had curled his little fist around Justice's finger and that tiny, fierce grip had taken hold of him more deeply than he would have thought possible.

The exercise-and-massage sessions Maggie had devised were getting less tiring as he healed, and he both hated that fact and was relieved by it. One-on-one time with Maggie was dangerous because he wanted her now more than ever. He hated missing those moments, but he also needed the space to do some serious thinking. Once the paternity test results came in, he would know if Maggie had been lying to him all this time. He would know if the baby boy he was becoming more fond of every day was his son.

And he would know what he had to do.

If Maggie was lying, then he'd have to let her go again. No matter how much he still loved her, no matter how much he'd come to care for the boy, he wouldn't be used. By anyone. But even as he thought it, a voice in his head shouted at him that it wasn't in Maggie's nature to lie. She was as forthright and honest a person as he'd ever known.

Which meant that as far as she knew, she was telling the absolute truth. Jonas was his son. If the tests proved it out, then Justice was going to be a part of the boy's life, whether or not Maggie was happy about that.

However the chips fell, he and Maggie had some tough choices headed their way. So why clutter everything up further with sex?

"Hey, boss!"

Justice turned toward the voice and spotted Mike leading one of the young horses around the perimeter of the ring. "What?"

Mike pointed toward the house. "Looks like your boy there is a born ranch hand!"

Justice swiveled his head to look and saw Maggie and Jonas on the flagstone patio. She was kneeling beside Jonas, who sat astride a rocking horse that had been in the King family for decades. Mrs. Carey must have hauled it down from the attic, Justice mused, a smile on his face as he watched Jonas hold on to the reins and rock unsteadily, his mother's arm wrapped firmly around him.

Even from a distance, he heard the baby's delighted laugh and Maggie's soft chuckle, and the mingled sounds went straight to his heart. If she was lying, how the hell was Justice going to stand losing her and the baby?

Nine

Maggie was putting her laundry away when she noticed the corner of a brown envelope peeking out from beneath a stack of T-shirts.

The signed divorce papers.

She set the laundry down, reached into the drawer for the large manila envelope and carefully opened the metal tabs. Pulling the papers free, she let her gaze drift over the legalese that would have, if she'd only filed the damn things with the court, ended her marriage.

But then, that was the problem. Despite going

to the trouble of getting the papers, of having Justice sign them, Maggie never really had wanted the marriage to be over. So now, she simply kept the signed documents with her. As a sort of talisman, she supposed. As long as she had them, she was still connected to Justice. Jonas still had a father. And she had a chance at getting back what she and Justice had lost. Was she just fooling herself, though? Torturing herself with thoughts of reconciliation?

Sex between them was still off-the-charts great. But was that it? Was that all they shared now?

Sadly, she slid the papers back into the envelope, then dropped the package back into her drawer. Turning from the dresser, she walked to the open window overlooking the front of the house and stared out at the storm blowing in off the ocean.

The white sheers at the window billowed in the wind gusting in under the sash like ghosts fighting to be free of earth. Tree limbs clat-

tered and seagulls wheeled and danced in the
sky, taking refuge inland from the approach-
ing storm. She closed the window against the
cold wind and told herself firmly that when
she got back to her own apartment, she had to
file those divorce papers. But even as she
thought it, she knew she wouldn't do it.

"You're crazy, Maggie," she whispered.

"I always liked that about you."

She spun around quickly, hand splayed
across her chest as if to keep her heart in place.
"Nothing like a jolt of adrenaline to get the
morning off to a great start."

"Didn't mean to startle you," Justice said as
he walked into her room with slow, but even
steps. "Thought you would have heard me
coming down the hall."

She watched him as he moved without hesitating, or limping. He was nearly back to
normal and hadn't used his cane in a couple
of days. Soon, he wouldn't need her at all.
Well, wasn't that a cheery thought?

"No, without the tapping of the cane giving you away, you're pretty stealthy."

He nodded, reached down to rub his thigh and said, "It's good to be rid of it."

"I'm sure it is." She moved back to the dresser and tucked her laundry into the proper drawers, then straightened, gave him a bright smile and said, "Well, I really should go down and get Jonas. Mrs. Carey's had him most of the morning."

"It can wait another minute." He moved to stand between her and the door and Maggie knew the only way she'd get past him was to brush up against him. And she didn't think that was a good idea. Not since her body remembered their time in the hot tub all too well and was just itching for more.

So instead she stopped, hitched one hip higher than the other and folded her arms over her chest. "Okay. What do you need, Justice?"

His gaze locked on hers, he said, "I think it's

time you and I had a talk about what's going to happen when the test results come in."

"What do you mean?" Wariness crept into her voice, but she really couldn't help it.

"I mean, in a few days we'll know the truth. And if it turns out that Jonas really is my son…"

She bristled. God, she hated that he didn't trust her and instead needed substantiating proof from a laboratory.

"—then I'm going to want him raised here," Justice was saying and Maggie listened up. "On the ranch."

A sinking sensation opened up in the pit of her stomach and her heart dropped into it. She shook her head. "No way."

"What?"

"You can't just take my son."

"If he's my son, too," Justice argued, "I can take my share of him."

She laughed shortly, a harsh scrape against her throat. "What do you plan to do? Cut him in half?"

He scowled and walked past her to sit on the edge of the bed. Rubbing his leg, he said, "Nothing so dramatic. If Jonas is mine, I want him raised here. I want him growing up where I did. This ranch is his heritage, and he should get to know it and love it like I do."

"All of a sudden you're worried about his *heritage?*" Maggie stalked across the floor toward him and stopped just before she got within strangling range. Because the way she was feeling at the moment, she really didn't trust herself. "Up until last week you wouldn't even admit to the possibility of his being your son. Now he has a heritage and you want to take him from me? I don't think so."

"Don't fight me on this, Maggie," Justice said, wincing a little as if his leg was paining him. "You'll lose."

For the first time since she'd arrived at the ranch, she wasn't concerned with Justice's pain. With the discomfort of his injury. In fact, she hoped his leg ached like a bitch. Why should she be the only one in pain here? All she knew was that he was going to take her baby from her. Well, it would have to be over her dead body.

She took a deep breath, held on to her heartache like a shield and said, "Oh, no, I won't lose. He's mine, Justice. He's nearly six months old and up until little more than a week ago, you'd never seen him!"

"Because you didn't bother to tell me of his existence."

"You didn't believe me when I *did* tell you."

"Not the point." He waved that argument aside with a flick of his hand.

"It's exactly the point, Justice, and you know it."

Outside, clouds rolled in, the wind kicked up into a fierce dance and rain suddenly pounded on the windowpanes with a vicious rhythm.

Feeling as ragged and frenetic as the storm, Maggie stepped back from him and said firmly, "Jonas is going to be raised in the city.

By me. My apartment is lovely. There's a park close by and good schools and—"

"A park?" Justice pushed off the bed and grimaced a little but kept coming, walking toward Maggie until she backed up just to keep a distance between them. "You want to give him a park when I've got thousands of acres here? The city's no place for a boy to grow up. He couldn't even have a *dog* in your apartment."

"Of course he can," she argued, temper spiking, desperation growing. "Pets are allowed in my building. We'll get a little dog as soon as he's old enough. A poodle, maybe."

He barked out a sharp laugh. "A *poodle?* What the hell kind of dog is that for a growing boy?"

"What do you want him to have, a pit bull?"

"The herd dogs. They're well-trained—he'll love 'em. We've got a new litter due in a few weeks, too. He'll have a puppy to grow up with and he'll love that, too."

He probably would, but that wasn't the point either, Maggie thought, surrendering to the fires inside her, letting her temper boil until she wouldn't have been surprised to feel steam coming out of her own ears.

"That's not your decision to make."

"Damn straight it is. If Jonas is my son, I won't be separated from him."

"You never even *wanted* children, remember?" She was shouting now and didn't give a damn who heard her. The rain hammered the windows, the wind rattled the glass and Maggie felt as if she were in the center of the storm. This was a fight she was determined to win. She wouldn't give ground.

"Of course I did!" Justice's shout was even louder than hers. "I lied to you because I thought I couldn't have kids."

Dumbfounded, Maggie just stared at him for a second or two. A heartbeat passed, then another, as her brain clicked through information and presented her with a really infuriating picture. Eventually that temper kicked back in and all hell was cut loose.

"You lied to me?" she demanded. "Deliberately let me believe you just didn't want kids when you knew you couldn't have them at all? Why would you do that?"

She rushed him and pushed at his chest with both hands, so furious she could hardly breathe, let alone shout, yet somehow she managed. "You let me walk away from you rather than tell me the truth? What were you thinking?"

"I didn't want you to know," he said, capturing both of her wrists and holding them tightly. His gaze pierced into hers, and Maggie saw shame and anger and regret all tangled up together in his eyes. "I didn't want anyone to know. You think I wanted to tell you I was less than a man?"

Maggie just blinked at him. She couldn't believe this. Couldn't get her mind around it at all. "Are you a Neanderthal? Being able to father a child is not a measure of your manhood, you big dolt!"

"To me it is."

She saw the truth of that statement on his face, and it didn't calm her down any. Yanking her hands free of his grip, she wheeled around and started pacing the circumference of the room in fast, furious steps.

"All this time, we've been apart because you thought you were sterile?" She sent him a quick look and saw her words hit home.

His mouth tightened, his jaw clenched and every muscle in his body looked to be rigid, unforgiving. He didn't accept weakness, and of course that's how he would have seen himself. She knew that about him if nothing else. So, yes, she could understand that he would have thought it better to get a divorce than to confess to his wife that he was less than he thought he should be.

That's what she got for marrying a man whose pride was his major motivator. How typical of Justice. Then she stopped dead, studied her husband and hit him with what she'd just realized.

"It's your damn pride, isn't it?" she murmured, never taking her eyes off him. "That's what's at the bottom of all this. Why you didn't fight for me. Why you let me go. For the sake of your damn pride."

"Nothing wrong with pride, Maggie," he told her in a voice that just barely carried over the sound of the storm raging outside.

"Unless you hold that pride more precious than anything else. Because that's what you did, Justice. Rather than admit to me you couldn't have children, you let our marriage end." The slap of that truth hurt her deeply. He'd chosen his own image of himself over their marriage. Over their love. "*That* was easier for you than losing your pride."

"You're the one who walked."

"So you keep reminding me," she said, moving back toward him now with slow, sure steps. "But you could have kept me, Justice. You could have stopped me with two words. *Please stay.* That's all you had to say and you know it. Hell, you admitted to me just the other day that you would have liked to say it. But you couldn't do it."

She shook her head as she stared up into dark blue eyes that suddenly looked as cold and deep as a storm-tossed ocean. "I loved you enough that I would have stayed with you if I thought you wanted me to. Instead you pulled away and closed yourself off and I had nothing. No children. No husband. So why the hell would I stay?"

He flinched and looked uncomfortable, but that was fleeting. In a heartbeat, he was back to being his stone-faced, in-control self.

"This is useless, Maggie." He pushed one hand through his hair, cast a quick look at the window and the storm beyond, then shifted his gaze back to her. "What's past is past. We can't change it. But know this. If Jonas is my son, I'm not going to give him up. If that boy is a King, he's going to be raised by Kings."

He left her then, walking quietly away without a backward glance, and when he was gone, Maggie felt cold right down to the bone. That icy pit in the bottom of her stomach was still there and now tangled with knots of nerves.

Everything Justice had just said had also been motivated by his pride, his pride in his child, and while she might ordinarily cheer for that, right now all it meant to her was that Justice would be a fierce opponent.

As that thought flew through her mind, Maggie realized that with his money and his family's power behind him, he might very well roll right over her and win custody if it ever went to court. Then what would she do?

She couldn't lose her son.

Everything in her went cold and still. Fear rocketed through her system, successfully dousing the fires of her temper.

This was so much more dangerous than she'd ever thought.

* * *

"I'll run away. I swear I will," Maggie said into the phone a half hour later. "I'll take Jonas and disappear."

"Calm down, sweetie," Matrice urged her. "Now just tell me what happened without the hysterics, okay?"

Sitting on her bed, watching her son stare out the window at the play of the storm outside, Maggie went over her whole fight with Justice. She told her elder sister everything, sparing neither of them, and by the time she was finished talking, she had to admit she felt better already, just for the spewing factor.

"I can't believe he'd be that dumb," Matrice said. "If he'd just told you the truth before, none of this would have happened."

"I already covered that, believe me," Maggie told her and smiled when Jonas kicked his little legs as if he were desperately trying to get up and run.

"I know, but, oh, hold on—" She half

covered the mouthpiece so that her voice was muffled as she said, "Danny, don't pour oatmeal on the cat, honey. That's a bad choice. Sorry," she told Maggie when she was back. "We're getting a late start on breakfast and Danny apparently wants to share."

Maggie smiled, thinking of her almost two-year-old nephew. The little boy attacked each day as if determined to get as much out of it as he could. Maggie could hardly wait to watch Jonas at that age. She looked down at her son, trying to grab hold of his own toes, and smiled. There was so much to look forward to. So much she could lose if Justice meant what he said and actually tried to take her son.

Fear galloped along her spine and Maggie took a deep breath, trying to rein it in.

"Mags? You there?" Matrice's voice brought Maggie back to earth and grounded her in the present.

Her older sister was matter-of-fact and down-to-earth, and she had enough common sense to talk Maggie off the proverbial ledge when she had to. Today, that talent was essential.

"I'm here, Matrice. Worried and a little nauseous, but I'm here."

"You don't have to worry."

"Easy for you to say."

Matrice laughed. "Honey, I'd be worried, too, if I actually believed that Justice would take you to court over your son."

"What makes you think he won't?"

"Because I'm brilliant and insightful. That's why you called me, remember?"

True. But still, Matrice hadn't seen Justice's face. His stern, determined expression.

"It's not going to go to court, I promise you, so relax a little, okay?"

"You don't know that," Maggie assured her, reaching out to smooth her hand across her son's inky black hair and skim her fingertips along his cheek. Instantly, Jonas made a grab for her finger and held on, as if he'd caught a prize. He couldn't possibly realize that he also had a grip on his mother's heart. "Justice is single-minded if nothing else, remember? And now that he's focused on Jonas and being a part of his life, there's nothing that will stop him. He'll do whatever he has to, to ensure he wins."

"But he can't win if he alienates you, and he knows it."

"Maybe. But he's so focused on Jonas."

Matrice chuckled. "That's not a bad thing, honey. You *wanted* him in Jonas's life, remember? That was one of the reasons you took the job when Jeff offered it. You wanted Justice to get to know his son. To want to be in his life."

"Yeah…" Okay, yes, that had been the plan. "But I didn't mean for him to take my son from me."

"He's not going to."

"You can't be sure of that."

"Yes, I can."

"How?" Maggie asked, really wanting to be convinced.

Her sister sighed into the phone. "Justice loves you, Mags. He always has. He wouldn't hurt you like that, and if you think about it, you'll see that's true."

"Yes, but…"

"And please, he's going to take the baby from you? Can you see him raising a baby on his own? It would be pitiful. Why, my own Tom hardly knows which end of the diaper goes under Danny's behind!"

"True," Maggie said, smiling now as her nerves began to unwind a little. She remembered the still-awkward way Justice held his son and knew that he'd be lost if he had to take care of the baby on his own. Then something occurred to her. "But he has Mrs. Carey and she's crazy about Jonas!"

"She's crazy about you, too," Matrice insisted. "No way would that woman help Justice take your son from you."

"Maybe not," she said with a sigh, lifting her gaze from the grinning baby to the stormy skies beyond the window. "But, Matrice, I can't help thinking this is going to get uglier before it gets any better."

"My money's on you, kid," her sister said.

A few hours later Justice studied the ranch report spread out on his desk, but he couldn't keep his mind from wandering. He'd put a call into King Labs and was unable to get an answer from them yet. What the hell was taking so long? Why couldn't they just finish the damn test and end the waiting?

He leaned back in his chair then, willing to admit at least to himself that his mind wasn't on the ranch. Instead, it was tangled up with thoughts of Maggie and the boy who might be his son. And if he wasn't? he asked himself. What then? Then, he thought, Maggie would leave, taking Jonas with her, and life at the ranch would once again be quiet as the grave.

Was he really willing to go back to living like that?

Justice scrubbed both hands over his face. No, he wasn't. He hated the idea of once more being alone in this house but for Mrs. Carey. He didn't like the idea of not seeing toys everywhere. Of not hearing the baby cry or Maggie's laughter ringing through the halls.

But did he have a choice? Had there been too many lies to patch up a marriage that had once been so shining and right? Great sex wasn't enough. Not when there had been so many harsh words between a couple. Not when distrust roared up at every corner. And, as he'd told himself before, great sex only complicated things. Remembering the look on her face when he'd finally confessed the truth to her, Justice had to acknowledge that maybe what they'd once shared was too shattered to put back together. And if their marriage was really over, what was left?

A small boy who would need both of them.

He accepted that if Jonas wasn't his, then Maggie was lying to him. But hadn't he lied to her, too? Hadn't he done just what she'd accused him of doing—chosen his pride over their marriage? Was her lie so much more terrible than his? Would it be so bad to accept another man's child as his own?

People adopted every day. Why couldn't he?

Warming to his thoughts, Justice stood up and walked to the wide windows overlooking the ranch yard. The storm was still raging, matching the way he was feeling exactly. He laid one hand on the cold glass and felt the tiny slaps of the rain as the drops bounced against his palm.

All he had to do was accept Jonas and he would have an heir. He'd have a boy he could raise and teach. Did it really matter who had created him as long as Justice raised him?

A small voice in his mind whispered *yes, it matters.* And his pride stirred and did battle with his desires. He couldn't ask her to be his wife again. That was done. Maggie and he might be finished, but they could have something different, he thought now. Something less than a marriage, less than lovers and more than friendship. It could work.

He could have Maggie *and* a son if he was willing to bend.

The question was, could he?

When the study door opened behind him, Justice didn't even have to turn around to know she was there. Watching him. He felt the power of her gaze and waited for her to approach. Her steps were muffled against the thick rugs spread across the wood floor, but he heard her anyway. That sure, confident step was purely Maggie.

She stopped directly behind him, and he could have sworn he felt the heat of her body reaching out for his.

"I won't lose my son, Justice," she said, and though her voice was quiet, there was a ring of steel in her tone.

He admired that. Hell, he'd always admired Maggie. Justice turned around to face her, and his gaze swept her up and down, noting the faded jeans, the cream-colored sweater and the wild tangle of her fiery hair. Her blue eyes were calm and fixed on him, but her chin was lifted into fighting mode and he knew she was ready to draw a line in the sand.

So he cut her off before she could.

"You don't have to," he said and saw the brief flash of confusion on her face. "I've been thinking about this since this morning, and an idea just came to me."

She tipped her head to one side to watch him warily. "What kind of idea?"

He leaned back against the window jamb, folded his arms across his chest and said, "I want you to move back to the ranch. You and Jonas."

"You mean once the test results are in."

"No," he said. "I mean now."

She shook her head as if she didn't quite understand what he was saying. And hell, who could blame her.

"But you don't even believe that Jonas is yours yet."

"Doesn't matter," he said and actually felt the ring of truth in that statement resonate in his soul. He'd made up his mind. Jonas would be his. Biologically or legally. "I can adopt him legally. Either way, he'll still be my son."

"I see," she said, though he was guessing she really didn't, since her features were carefully blank. "So, you want me to move back in as your wife?"

Step carefully, King, he told himself.

"No," he said quietly, "we're divorced and that's probably best. Maggie, we were always too combustible for our own good. I know our marriage is over. But there's no reason you can't move in here anyway. We can raise Jonas together and have a platonic relationship."

Her jaw dropped.

He smiled. It wasn't easy to surprise Maggie King.

"*Platonic?*" She repeated the word as if she

couldn't quite believe he'd actually said it. "Whatever we have together, Justice, it's never been platonic."

"Doesn't mean it can't be," he countered. God knew, he wouldn't enjoy it much, but if that's what it took to have her and the baby in his world, then that's what he'd do. "We could have a good life, Maggie. We'd be close… friends."

"We'll never be just friends, Justice," she told him. "Don't you get that? There's too much between us. Too much passion to be stoppered up in a jar and set on a shelf somewhere to make things easier for you."

"You're taking this all the wrong way, Maggie. That's not what I'm trying to do."

"Isn't it?" She pushed both hands through her hair and growled briefly under her breath as if she were trying to get hold of her temper. "You've decided Jonas will be your son whether he is or not. You've decided that I can be your friend and live here at the ranch. But you're not saying anything about trying for something more, because Justice King doesn't make mistakes."

"What the hell are you talking about?"

"Don't you think I know what you're doing?" She laughed then, hard and fast. "God, I know you even better than you know yourself. You won't ask me to live with you as your wife again because that would mean you made a mistake when you let me leave you. And you don't make mistakes, do you, Justice?"

He just stared at her. How was a man supposed to unravel the wild logic women came up with? "How the hell did you twist this around like that?"

"Because I know you." She laughed shortly and shook her head while she waved one finger at him. "You don't want platonic, Justice, any more than I do. You just figure that's the easiest way to get me to agree. Then, once I'm living here at the ranch, you can change things. You've probably got it all planned out in your mind. I can just see it," she continued, wiggling her fingers in wide circles that got smaller and smaller. "You'll work it around to the arrangement that will suit you best. And what suits you, Justice, is me in your bed. You want *me*. You want our bodies tangled together. You want hot breath and soul-stealing kisses."

He took a long, slow breath and then swallowed hard. Figured Maggie would make this more difficult than it had to be. Figured she would see right through his "platonic" offer, too. The woman always had been way too smart. "Of course I want you—that's obvious enough—but it doesn't mean we can't live as friends."

"Oh, of course it does. It would be impossible. You and I, Justice, were never meant for platonic." Then she went up on her toes, wrapped her arms around his neck and pulled him in for a long, deep kiss that held as much fury as passion.

Justice would have sworn he felt heat swamp him from the top of his head to the bottoms of his feet. She was fire and light and heat and seduction. His arms snaked around her middle, held on tight and pressed her to him, aligning her body to his. He was tight and hard for her in an instant and knew she was making her point all too well.

Then the kiss was over and she was looking up into his eyes. "Deny that, if you can. We're not friends. We're lovers." Her arms dropped from around his neck. "Or we were. Now, I'm not sure what we are anymore. The only thing I'm sure of is, I won't lose my son."

She turned her back on him and stomped out of the room without once looking back. But why should she? She'd made her point.

His arms felt empty without her in them. His body was on fire and slowly cooling now that Maggie was gone. Damn it, he hated the cold. He wanted the heat. He wanted *her*. And he always would. She was right. They couldn't live together as friends. So what did that leave them?

They had a past.

They might have a future.

All it would cost him was his pride.

Ten

"**Y**ou're as stubborn as he is, I swear." Mrs. Carey gave her soup pot a stir, then fisted her hands at her hips. "That poor baby is going to have a head like a rock thanks to his parents."

Maggie sat at the kitchen table, drinking tea she didn't want and staring through the window at Justice as he carried Jonas around the ranch yard. Spring sunshine fell out of a perfect sky. Angel and Spike were racing in circles, making Jonas laugh with delight, and the wide grin on Justice's face stole her breath away.

Yet here she sat in the kitchen. It was a bright, cheery room, with dozens of cabinets, miles of countertop and the comforting scent of homemade soup bubbling on the stove. But Maggie didn't feel comforted. More like… disconnected.

At the end of a very long week, she felt as though she were walking a tightwire fifty feet off the ground with no net beneath her. Days crawled past and she and Justice might as well have been living in separate homes. She hadn't touched him in days, though she'd dreamed about him every night. Thought about him every waking moment.

And still there didn't seem to be an answer.

"What am I supposed to do?" Maggie asked with a shake of her head. "He wants us to be *friends*."

Mrs. Carey snorted. "Anyone can see you two weren't destined for friendship."

Smiling wryly, Maggie said, "I agree, but what if that's all that's left to us?"

Mrs. Carey walked to the table, sat down opposite her and folded her hands neatly on top of a brick-red placemat. Staring Maggie in the eyes, she asked bluntly, "If all that's left is friendship, why does the air sizzle when the two of you are together?"

Maggie laughed. "Excuse me?"

"Do I look like I'm a hundred and fifty years old?" Mrs. Carey snorted again and clucked her tongue. "Because I'm not. And anyone with half an eye could have seen the way you two were around each other the past couple of weeks. I nearly caught fire myself, just watching the two of you look at each other."

No point in denying the truth, Maggie thought. So she didn't try. "Not lately, though."

"No," Mrs. Carey allowed. "What I've got to wonder is why? What changed?"

"What hasn't?" Reaching for a cookie from the plate in the center of the table, Maggie took a bite, chewed, then swallowed. "He wants Jonas, but he hasn't said he wants *me*."

"Pfft." The older woman waved away that statement with one dismissive hand. "You know he does."

"What I know and what I need to hear are two different things," Maggie said, letting her gaze slide once again to the two most important men in her life. She looked out the window just in time to see Justice plant a kiss on Jonas's forehead.

Her heart melted. She'd wished for this for so long, that Justice would know and love his son, and now it was happening. The only problem was that she should have been more specific in her wishes. She should have hoped that the *three* of them would find one another.

"Maggie, you more than anybody know that Justice doesn't always say what he's feeling," Mrs. Carey said softly, drawing her gaze away from the window. "You love him. I can see it in you."

"Yeah, I love him," she admitted. "But that doesn't change anything."

The other woman laughed. "Oh, honey. It changes everything. With love, anything's possible. You just can't give up."

"I'm not the one giving up," she retorted, defending herself. "Justice is the one who won't budge."

"Hmm…"

"What's that mean?"

"Nothing at all," Mrs. Carey said with a sigh. "Just seems to me that people as stubborn as you and Justice have an obligation to the world to stick together. Spare two other people from having to put up with either of you."

She had to laugh. One thing about Justice's housekeeper, you never had to wonder what she was thinking.

"Now, why don't you go outside and join your men?"

She wanted to. She really did. But things were so strained between Justice and her at the moment that she wasn't at all sure she'd be welcomed. Besides, now that Justice was almost back to full strength, she'd be leaving soon and taking Jonas with her, no matter what the baby's father thought about it. So why not let the two of them have some time together while they could?

But, oh, the thought of leaving the ranch again, leaving *Justice* again, was killing her. And the fear that he might make good on his promise and try to take her son was chilling. Pain was gathering on the near horizon, and she knew that when it finally caught up to her, it was going to be soul crushing.

"No," Maggie said, standing up slowly. It was time she started getting used to the fact that she wasn't going to be with Justice. Brace for the coming pain as best she could. "I think I'll go upstairs, take a long bath and start getting ready for tonight."

Mrs. Carey nodded. "It's good that you're going with him."

Maybe it was, Maggie thought, but maybe it would turn out to be an exercise in torture for both of them. She'd agreed days ago to attend the Feed the Hungry charity dance with Justice.

Feed the Hungry was a local foundation the King Ranch donated hundreds of thousands of dollars every year to in order to stock local food banks. Maggie had even helped plan the event when she and Justice were still together. So attending with him had seemed like a good idea when he'd first broached the subject.

But now…she wasn't so sure. Looking down at the woman still seated at the table, she asked, "Are you certain you don't mind babysitting while we go? Because if you do, I can stay home and—"

"It's a joy to watch that baby, and you well know it," Mrs. Carey told her with a smile. "So if you're thinking of chickening out at the last minute, you can't use me as an excuse."

Maggie's lips twitched. "Some friend you are."

"Honey, I am your friend. And as your friend, I'm telling you to go upstairs. Take a bath. Do your hair and makeup and wear that gorgeous dress you bought yesterday." She stood up, came around the table and gave Maggie a brief, hard hug. "Then you go out with your husband. Dance. Talk. And maybe remember just what it is you two have together before it's too late."

Justice hated getting dressed up.

He felt uncomfortable in the tailored tux and wished to hell he was wearing jeans and his boots. He even had a headache from gathering up his hair and tying it into a neat ponytail at the back of his neck. He didn't get why it mattered what he wore to this damn thing. Why couldn't he just write a check and be done with it?

Scowling, he glanced around the hallway and noted that the cobalt blue vase held a huge bouquet of roses, their scent spilling through the entryway. Now that Maggie was back on the ranch, the vases were filled again; he knew that when she was gone, it would be just one more thing he would miss. She'd made her mark on this place as well as on him. And nothing would be the same after she left.

His leg was better now, so he knew that she'd be planning to go soon. He couldn't let that happen. Not this time. He had to find a way to make her stay. Not just because of Jonas but also because without Maggie, Justice didn't feel complete.

He shot his cuffs, checked his watch and frowned. Maggie always had kept him waiting. Back in the day, he'd stood at the bottom of these steps, hollering up for her to get a move on, and she'd always insisted that she would be worth the wait.

"Damned if that isn't still true," he murmured when he spotted her at the top of the stairs.

Her long, red-gold hair fell loosely around her shoulders, the way he liked it best. Long, dangling gold earrings glittered and shone in the light tossed from a wall sconce. She wore a strapless, floor-length dark green dress that clung to her curves until practically nothing was left to the imagination. The bodice was low-cut, exposing the tops of her breasts, and the skirt fell in graceful folds around her legs. She carried a black cashmere wrap folded neatly across her arm.

She stood there, smiling at him, and his breath caught in his lungs. Her cheeks were pink and her blue eyes sparkled as she enjoyed his reaction to her. If she only knew just how strong his response was. Suddenly, his tux felt even more uncomfortable than it had before as his body tightened and pushed at the elegant fabric.

"Well?" she asked, making a slow turn at the top of the stairs.

Justice hissed in a breath. The back was cut so low she was practically naked. The line of her spine drew his gaze, and he followed it down to the curve of her behind, just barely hidden by the green silk. His hands itched to touch her. It took everything he had to keep from vaulting up the stairs—bad leg or not—crushing her to him and carrying her off to the closest bed.

She'd been right, he told himself. They weren't friends. They'd never *be* friends. He wanted her desperately and doubted that feeling would ever fade.

But she was waiting for him to say something, watching him now with steady eyes. He didn't disappoint her.

"You're beautiful," he whispered, his voice straining to be heard past the knot in his throat. "Every man in the room is going to want you."

She came down the stairs slowly, one hand on the banister, each step measured and careful. He got peeks of her sandaled feet as she moved and noticed a gold toe ring he'd never paid attention to before. Sexy as hell, he thought, and grimly fought a losing battle to get his own body back under control.

"I'm not interested in every man," she said when she was just a step or two above him.

"Good thing," he told her. "I'd hate to have to bring a club to fight them off with."

She gave him a dazzling smile that sent his heartbeat into overdrive.

"I think that's the nicest thing you've ever said to me, Justice."

Then he'd been a damn fool, he thought. He should have always told her how beautiful she was. How important to him she was. But he hadn't found the words and so he'd lost her. Maybe, though, there was time enough for him to take another shot at it.

He reached out, took one of her hands in his and helped her down the last two steps. When she was standing right in front of him, he inhaled, drawing her scent into his body as if taking all of her in. He lifted one hand, smoothed her hair back from her cheek, touched her cool, soft skin and felt only fire.

"Maggie, I—"

"Well, now, don't you both look wonderful," Mrs. Carey said as she walked into the hall, Jonas on her hip.

Justice didn't know if he was relieved or irritated by the interruption.

The baby kicked his legs, waved his arms and, with drool streaming down his chin, reached for his mother. Maggie moved to take him, but Mrs. Carey stepped back. "Oh, no, you don't," she said, laughing. "He'll have you covered in drool in no time—you don't want to ruin that dress."

Maggie sighed and Justice watched her eyes warm as she looked at her son. He felt it, too, he realized, looking at the baby safe in the housekeeper's arms. A wild, huge love for a tiny child he wasn't even sure was his yet. But the more time he spent with the baby, the more he saw of him, the more he cared for him. He and Maggie were linked through this child, he knew. But would it be enough to start over? To rebuild what they'd lost?

"She's right," he said, keeping a tight grip on Maggie's hand. "We're late anyway."

Maggie lifted one eyebrow at him. "Was that a dig?"

He gave her a half smile. "Just a fact. You always did make us late for everything."

"I like to make an entrance."

"You do a hell of a job, I'll give you that," he said and was rewarded by a quick grin. Her smile sucker punched him, and he had to steady himself again before looking at Mrs. Carey. When he did, he found the older woman giving him a knowing look. She saw too much for Justice's comfort. Always had.

"Goodnight, little man," Maggie whispered as she leaned in to Jonas and kissed his cheek. Then she cupped her hand around the back of his head and just held on to him for a long moment. Pulling back, then she said, "Does he feel a little warm to you?"

"Warm?" Justice repeated, reaching out to place his palm on the baby's forehead, a sudden, sharp stab of worry slicing through him. "You think he has a fever?"

"Maybe we should check before we go," Maggie said. "It won't take long and—"

"He'll be fine—don't you worry." Mrs. Carey shook her head at both of them. "I know how to take care of a baby and if I need you, I'll call your cell."

"You've got the number, right?" Maggie asked, digging in her small cocktail purse to drag out her cell phone and make sure it was on.

"Of course I do, you've given it to me three times just today."

"My number's programmed on your phone, too, right?" Justice asked, patting his pants pocket to assure himself he had his phone, as well.

"I have your number, too. And the police," Mrs. Carey said, herding them toward the front door. "And the hospital and probably the National Guard. Go. Dance. Have fun."

Frowning a little at the bum's rush they were

receiving, Justice took hold of Maggie's elbow and steered her onto the porch. "We're going, but we're only a few miles away and—"

"I know where Stevenson Hall is, Justice. Haven't I lived here most of my life?" Mrs. Carey shooed them off with one hand. "Go on, have some fun, for heaven's sake. The baby's fine and he's going to stay fine."

"If you're sure…" Maggie didn't sound at all pleased about leaving now and her gaze was fixed on the smiling baby.

"Go."

Justice took Maggie's wrap from her, draped it over her bare shoulders, then took her arm and threaded it through his. Giving his housekeeper one more look, he said, "She's right. Jonas will be fine, and if we have to, we can be back home in ten minutes."

"All right, then," Maggie said unenthusiastically. She looked at Mrs. Carey. "You promise to call me if he needs me?"

"Absolutely," she said. "Drive safe."

Then she closed the door and Maggie and Justice were standing on the dimly lit porch all alone. Her scent drifted to him and the heat of her body called to him—and Justice could only think he'd never been less interested in going anywhere. It wasn't worry over the baby making him want to stay home. It was the idea of having this elegantly dressed, absolutely beautiful Maggie King all to himself.

But he had an obligation to the charity the King Ranch funded, so he would go. "We don't have to stay long," he said, leading her down the porch and across the drive to where one of the ranch hands had parked the SUV.

"I know." Maggie threw one last glance at the house behind her, then turned to look at Justice. "Jonas is probably fine, and besides, I want a dance with a handsome man in a tux tonight."

His mouth quirked slightly. "Anyone I know?"

She laughed as he'd meant her to, then said, "Maybe Mrs. Carey is right. Maybe we should try to relax and enjoy the night."

"Maybe," he said, sliding one hand down her arm. "But for God's sake don't tell her that."

Maggie laughed again as she swung herself inside the car after he opened the door for her, and Justice told himself to enjoy what he had while he had it. He knew all too well just how quickly things could change.

The charity ball was a huge success.

The banquet hall at the local art center was packed with the county's movers and shakers. A band was playing dance music on the stage, and formally dressed waiters moved through the crowd carrying trays of appetizers. Helium-filled balloons in an array of colors filled the ceiling and occasionally fell limply to the floor below. Women dressed in jewel-toned gowns swirled in the arms of tuxedo-clad men, and Maggie was left to visit with friends instead of dancing with her husband as she wanted to.

She spotted Justice across the room,

standing in a knot of people. Even from a distance, her breath caught in her chest just watching him. He was magnificent in a tuxedo. She knew he hated formal wear, but even in a tux, his raw strength and sensuality bled through until most women would have had to fan themselves after a peek at him.

Maggie frowned when she saw him rub idly at his thigh. She probably should have put her foot down about attending this dance, but he was so damn proud. So reluctant to be treated as if he needed help. And the truth was, he was well on the way to being one hundred percent again, so a small ache or pain wasn't going to stop him anyway.

The men clustered around Justice were no doubt asking his advice on any number of things, she thought, while absentmindedly keeping track of the conversations around her. But that was how it had always been. People turned instinctively to Justice. He was a man who somehow gave off the air of being in complete control, and to most people that was simply irresistible.

She was no different. She looked at Justice and knew she wanted him with every breath in her body. He was the one. The only one for her. Sighing, she turned her head and smiled at the still-speaking woman beside her.

So when Justice came up behind her a moment or two later, she was so startled she jumped as he laid one hand on her back. Heat spilled through her as his fingers caressed her spine with a delicate touch. She closed her eyes, sighed a little and took a breath, hoping to regain her balance. Then, looking up at him, she asked, "Having a good time?"

He dipped his head to hers and murmured, "Hell, no, but it might get better if you dance with me."

Maggie smiled, then asked, "You sure you're up to it? Your leg, I mean."

"The leg's fine. A little achy." He held out

a hand. "So? A dance with the guy who brought you?"

"Oh, honey, if he was asking me to dance, I wouldn't hesitate." A few chuckles resulted from that statement by a woman old enough to be Justice's grandmother.

"Mrs. Barton," Maggie said with a teasing laugh, "you'd better be careful. I've got my eye on you."

As Justice led her through the crowd to the mobbed dance floor, Maggie felt a swell of pride inside her. There were any number of women in this room who would give anything to be on Justice's arm. And for tonight, at least, that woman was her.

She went into his arms as if it was the only place on earth she belonged. When he held her so tightly to him she could feel the strength of his body pressing into hers, Maggie nearly sighed with pleasure. Then he turned her lazily in time to the swell of the music, and she smiled, enjoying the moment. All around them, couples swayed in time and snatches of conversations lifted and fell in the air.

When Justice's step faltered, Maggie frowned. "Are you okay?"

He gritted his teeth. "I'm fine."

"We don't have to dance, Justice."

He hissed out a breath. "I said I'm fine, Maggie. The leg aches a little. That's all."

"I'm just concerned."

"You don't have to be, damn it," he ground out, then clamped his lips tightly together for a second before saying, "I don't need you to worry about me, all right? Can we just dance?"

But the magic of the moment was ruined for Maggie. *I don't need you.* His words repeated over and over again in her mind. "That's the problem, Justice," she blurted while still following his lead around the floor.

"What?" He was frowning again now, and damned if that expression didn't make him look more sexy. More dangerous.

"You don't need me."

"I said I don't need you to worry about me—there's a difference."

"No," she insisted, staring up at him as they made another turn. "There isn't. I need *you*. I always have."

"That's good, because—"

"No," she interrupted him, uncaring about the people surrounding them on the floor. They probably couldn't overhear the conversation over the music, but even if they could, that wouldn't have stopped her. "It isn't good, Justice. It's the reason I can't be with you."

"You *are* with me."

His hand tightened around hers and his eyes narrowed into slits. Maggie shook her head at his fierce expression. "Not for much longer. Yes, I need you, but I can't be with you, because I want to be needed, too."

"What the hell does that mean?" he demanded, holding her closer, as if half afraid she was going to bolt. "Of course I need you."

She laughed shortly, but there was no humor

in it, only misery. "No, you don't. You wouldn't even let me help you a second ago when your leg hurt."

"That's different, Maggie. I don't need a therapist."

"No," she said, her temper building, frothing, despite the fact that she was in the middle of a crowd that was slowly beginning to take notice. "You don't want to need anyone. You won't admit that you can't do everything yourself. It's your pride, Justice. It always comes down to your pride."

Justice's voice was low and tight. There were too many damn people around them. Too many who might be listening in. "My pride helped me build the ranch into one of the biggest in the country. My pride got me through when you walked out."

"Your pride is the *reason* I walked out, remember?"

"You're not walking this time," he told her, his grip on her hand and around her waist making that point clear. "This time we *have* to be together."

"Why?"

"Because I got a text from Sean at the lab. The results of the test are in. I'm Jonas's father."

Both of her eyebrows arched high on her forehead as she tried to pull free from his grasp. "If you're waiting for me to be surprised, don't bother."

"I know. I should have listened. I should have believed."

"Yes, you should have."

He felt as if a two-thousand-pound rock had been lifted off his shoulders. He felt change in the air, and it damn near made him laugh with the possibilities of it all. "Don't you get it, Maggie? This changes everything. I'm his father. That means the doctor was wrong. I *can* give you children."

"I already knew that, Justice," she said, glancing to the side as another couple moved in close.

"Which is why we're getting married," he said, the decision made and delivered like an order.

"Excuse me?" She stopped dancing, dragging him to a sudden halt.

"I said we're getting married."

Maggie frowned at someone who jostled her, then turned to him and announced, "I can't marry you. I'm already married."

"You're married?" Justice stared at her as if she were speaking Greek. "What do you mean you're *married?* We've been sleeping together!"

Several heads turned toward them now, and Justice scowled at the most obvious eavesdroppers, shaming them into looking away.

Maggie flushed right up to the roots of her hair, but it was fury, not embarrassment, staining her cheeks. "I'm married to *you,* Justice!"

She spun around on her heel and pushed her way through the crowd. Justice was left staring after her, stunned by her declaration and furious that he hadn't known about this before. He started after her, his steps long and sure. When he caught up with her, he grabbed her arm, turned her to face him and, ignoring the crowd, said, "I signed those divorce papers, Maggie! How the hell are we married?"

"I never filed them, you big jerk." And once again, she pulled free and made her way to the exit. Justice was right behind her, ignoring the wild rustle of conversations and laughter filling the hall behind him.

No doubt people would be talking about this night for a damn long time, he told himself while he took off after Maggie. Mostly, he suspected they'd be calling him a fool, and he'd have to agree.

He and Maggie were still married and he hadn't even known it. When he reached the front door, he raced outside and spotted Maggie walking with furious steps down the sidewalk in the direction of home. Racing for the parking lot, Justice found his car, started it up and chased down his errant wife.

Driving alongside her while she was muttering to herself and bristling with unleashed fury, he rolled down the passenger window and ordered, "Get in the car, Maggie."

"I don't *need* you, Justice." She made sure of the emphasis on the word *need,* and flipped her hair back behind her shoulders. "I'll walk."

"You can't walk it."

"Watch me."

"It's ten miles to the ranch."

She slowed a little, shot him a furious glare and said, "If I get in that car, don't you *dare* speak to me."

"We have to talk about this, Maggie."

"No, we don't. We've said plenty. In front of the whole town, no less. So if you can't promise me silence, I'll walk."

"You're freezing."

"I'm too mad to be cold."

"Damn it, Maggie!" He slammed on the

brakes, threw the car into Park and jumped
out, racing down the sidewalk to catch up to
her. His leg ached like a son of a bitch, but he
ignored the pulsing pain in his quest to catch
the most infuriating woman he'd ever known.
When he grabbed hold of her, he wasn't even
surprised to feel her turn into a hundred and
twenty pounds of fighting fury.

"Let me go, you big bully!" She wrenched
free from his grasp, and when his hand
clutched at her forearm again, she swung one
leg back to kick him in the shins. He dodged
that move and still didn't release her. "Don't
touch me. You humiliated me in front of the
whole town—"

His eyes went wide. "I humiliated *you?*"

"You told the whole damn room we've been
sleeping together."

"And you told 'em we're *married.* Who
cares?"

"I do, in case you haven't noticed."

"So, now whose pride is the problem?" That

one question delivered in a quiet, reasonable tone did what all of his arguments hadn't. They shut her up but fast, despite how resentful she looked about it.

"Fine. I'll take the ride. But I'm not talking to you, Justice. Not tonight. Not *ever.*"

He smiled to himself as he led her back to the car. One thing in this world he was sure of. Maggie Ryan King wouldn't be able to keep a vow of silence if her own life depended on it.

Eleven

By the time they reached the ranch, Maggie's temper had died into a slow burn. She could still see the shocked, delighted expressions on the faces of the people surrounding them at the ball. She just knew that by tomorrow the story was going to be all over the county.

And there wasn't a damn thing she could do about it. God, she felt like an idiot. She'd been harboring too many dreams about Justice, and seeing them shattered in an instant—in front of an audience—was just humiliating.

She had the door open and was jumping to the ground almost before the car had rolled to a stop.

"Damn it, Maggie! Wait a minute."

She ignored him and marched toward the house. She'd had enough. All she wanted now was to go inside, hug her baby and go to bed. Then when she woke up, she'd pack and get the heck out of Justice's house before he'd even had his morning coffee.

"Maggie, wait for me."

She glanced over her shoulder and hesitated when she saw him limp slightly. But a moment later, she reminded herself that he didn't want her help. He didn't need a therapist. He didn't need her.

Fumbling in her clutch purse for the front door key, she blew out a breath as Justice came up behind her, then reached past her to unlock the door and open it up.

"Thank you."

"You're welcome."

She hurried to the stairs, but his hand on her arm stopped her. "Maggie, at least talk to me."

Turning her gaze up to his, she stared into those dark blue eyes and felt a sigh slide from her throat. "What's left to say?"

"I'm so glad you're home. I was just getting ready to call you!"

They both turned to look up at the head of the stairs, where Mrs. Carey stood, holding a fretful Jonas. Instantly, Maggie gathered the hem of her dress, hiked it above her knees and raced up the stairs. Justice was just a step or two behind her.

Scooping her son into her arms, Maggie cuddled him close and inhaled sharply. "He's burning up!"

Justice came close, laid his hand on the back of Jonas's neck and shot a look at Mrs. Carey. "How long?"

She wrung her hands together. "He's been uneasy all night, but just in the past half hour or so, his fever's climbed. I tried calling the doctor but couldn't get him, so I was going to call you."

"It'll be fine, Mrs. Carey. Don't worry." He plucked Jonas from Maggie's arms and held him close to his chest. With his free hand, he took Maggie's and curled his fingers around hers. She immediately felt better, linked to his warmth and strength. When she looked up at him, she saw the calm, stoic expression she was used to.

Tonight, that was a comfort. She was so scared for Jonas that having Justice beside her, taking charge and looking confident, filled her with the same kind of certainty.

"We'll take him to the E.R.," Justice was saying, already starting down the stairs, taking Maggie with him.

"Don't you want to at least change clothes first?" Mrs. Carey called after them.

"Nope."

The emergency room in any city was a miserable place, Justice thought as he paced back and forth across the pale green linoleum. The smells, the sounds, the suffering, it all piled up on a person the minute he or she walked in the doors. They shouldn't have to be there. Kids shouldn't be allowed to get sick. There should be some sort of cosmic law against making a child who didn't even understand what was happening to him feel so bad. If he had his way, he thought, glancing over his shoulder to where Maggie sat on a gurney cradling Jonas in her lap, he'd see to it that his son was never in a place like this one again.

Everything in Justice tightened as he realized that what he was feeling was sheer terror with a thick layer of helplessness. And that was new. Justice had never in his life faced a situation that he couldn't fix—except for the time when Maggie had left him. Yet even then, he reminded himself, he could have stopped her if he'd let go of his own pride long enough to admit what was really important.

She'd been right, he realized. At the dance, when she'd accused him of letting their marriage dissolve because of his pride. But damn it, was a man supposed to lay down everything he was for the sake of the woman he loved?

Love.

That one word resonated inside him and seemed to echo over and over again. He loved her completely, desperately, and a life without her seemed like the worst kind of prison sentence.

His gaze fixed on Maggie now, he saw tears glimmering in her eyes. Saw her hand tremble as she stroked their son's back. Then she lifted her gaze to his, and he read absolute trust in those pale blue depths. She was looking to him to fix this. To make it right. She was turning to him despite the hard words and the hurt feelings that lay between them. Justice felt a stir of something elemental inside, and as he held her gaze, he swore to himself that he wouldn't let her down. And when this crisis with Jonas was past, he would do whatever he had to do to keep Maggie in his life.

As soon as they got Jonas taken care of and settled down in his own bed back at the ranch, he was going to tell her that he loved her. Tell her what she meant to him and how empty his life was without her—and his pride be damned.

"Justice, he feels so hot." She cradled the baby's head to her chest and rocked as Jonas sniffled and cried softly, rubbing tiny fists against his eyes.

His heart turned over as he watched the baby and reacted to Maggie's fears.

"I know," he said, "but don't worry, all right? Everything's gonna be fine, and I'm gonna get someone in here to see him even if I have to buy the damn hospital."

Someone out in the waiting room was crying, a moan came from behind a green curtain and nurses carrying clipboards hurried up and down a crowded hallway, their shoes squeaking on the floor. They'd been there an hour already, and but for a nurse checking Jonas's temperature when they first arrived, no one had come to check on the baby.

Maggie forced a smile. "I don't think buying the place is going to be necessary."

"It is if it's the only way I can get somebody's attention." He shot a glare over his shoulder at the hallway and the hospital beyond. "Damn it, he's a baby. He shouldn't have to wait as long as an adult."

Maggie sighed and smiled a little in spite of her obvious fear. "I'm glad you're here with me."

He stopped and stared at her. "You are?"

"God, yes," she said on a choked laugh. "I'd be a gibbering idiot right now if you weren't here with me, pacing in circles like a crazy person and threatening to buy hospitals."

He walked toward her and went into a crouch in front of her so that he could look at her and his son. He dragged the backs of his fingers across Jonas's too-warm cheek and felt a well of love fill his heart. The baby turned his head, looked at Justice and sighed. A tiny movement. A small breath. And dark blue eyes looking into his with innocence and confusion.

And in that instant, that one, timeless moment, Justice finally completed the fall into an overpowering love for his son. It had been coming on him for days, and maybe it was all instinctual. Like a cow in the spring that can pick out her own calf from the herd.

Nature, drawing families together, bonding them with an indefinable something that in humans was explained as love. A love so rich, so pure, so overwhelming, it nearly brought him to his knees. There was absolutely nothing on this earth that Justice wouldn't do for that boy. Nowhere he wouldn't go. Nothing he wouldn't dare.

"It'll be all right, son," he whispered, his voice breaking as his eyes misted over. "Your daddy's going to see to it."

Maggie reached for his hand and held on.

Linked together, a silent moment of complete understanding passed between them, and Justice couldn't help wondering how many other parents had been in this room. How many others had waited interminably for help.

"This is ridiculous," he said. "There should be more doctors. More nurses. People shouldn't have to wait. I swear, I'm going to talk to the city council. Hell, I'll donate an extra wing to this place and pay to see it's better staffed."

"Justice…"

"What the hell is taking so long?" he muttered, squeezing Maggie's hand to relieve his own impatience. "I don't get it. What do you have to do to get seen around here, bleed from an eyeball?"

"Well, wouldn't that be festive?" A woman's voice came from right behind him.

Justice whirled around to face a doctor, in her late fifties, maybe, with short, gray hair, soft brown eyes and an understanding smile on her face.

"I didn't see you."

"Clearly, and as to your earlier question, I'm sorry about the wait, but I'm here now. Let's take a look at your son, shall we?"

As the doctor walked past him toward the baby, she took the stethoscope off from around her neck and fitted the ear pieces into her ears. "Lay him down on the gurney, please," she said softly.

Maggie did but kept one hand on Jonas's belly, as if to reassure both of them. Justice stepped up behind her and laid one hand on her shoulder, linking the three of them together, into a unit.

"Let's just listen to your heart, little guy," the doctor crooned, giving Jonas a smile. She moved her stethoscope around the baby's narrow chest and made a note on a chart. Justice tried to read it but couldn't get a good look.

Then she checked his temperature and looked in his eyes. Finally, when the baby's patience evaporated and he let loose a wail, the doctor looked up and smiled.

"What is it? What's wrong with him?" Maggie reached to her shoulder to lay her hand over Justice's.

"Let me guess," the doctor said, hooking her stethoscope around her neck again before scooping Jonas up in capable hands and swaying to soothe his tears. "This is your first baby."

"Yes, but what does that have to do with anything?" Justice asked.

Jonas's tears had subsided, and he was suddenly fascinated by the doctor's stethoscope.

"Babies sometimes spike fevers," the doctor was saying. "Not sure why, really. Could be a new tooth. Could be he didn't feel well. Could be growing pains." Still smiling, she handed Jonas to his mother and looked from Maggie to Justice.

"The point is, he's fine. You have a perfectly healthy son." She checked her chart. "According to this, his temperature has already dropped. You can take him home, give him a tepid bath, it'll make him feel better. Then just keep an eye on him, and if you're worried about anything at all, you can either call me—" she wrote down a phone number on the back of her card "—or bring him back in."

Justice took the business card she handed him. He glanced at her name and nodded. "Thanks, Dr. Rosen. We appreciate it."

She grinned at him. "It's my pleasure. But if you meant what you were saying earlier, the hospital could use the extra wing and I've got lots of ideas."

Justice stared down at her and found himself smiling. There was so much relief coursing through his veins at the moment that he would have built the woman her own clinic if she'd asked him to. And he had the distinct feeling she knew it. As it was, he tucked her card into his breast pocket and said, "Give me a few days, and we'll talk about those ideas."

Her eyebrows shot straight up in surprise,

but she recovered quickly. "You've got a deal, Mr. King."

When she left, Maggie leaned in close to Justice and he slid his arms around her and their son, holding them tightly to him. He rested his chin on top of Maggie's head and took a long minute to simply enjoy this feeling.

He had his family in his arms, and there was simply no way he would lose them now.

The ride back to the ranch was quiet and Maggie was grateful.

There were too many thoughts whirling through her mind for her to be able to hold any kind of rational conversation. Behind her in his car seat, Jonas slept fretfully. Soft whimpers and sighs drifted to her, and she turned in her seat to look at him, needing to reassure herself that he was safe. And healthy.

When she faced the front again, she took a moment to study Justice's profile in the muted light from the dashboard. His eyes were fixed on the road ahead of them. His mouth was firm and tight, his jaw clenched as if he, too, were having trouble relaxing from the scare they'd had. In the shadows he looked fierce and proud and untouchable.

But the memory of his arms coming around her, holding her and the baby, was so strong and fresh in her mind that she knew he was right now hiding his emotions from her. Which was probably just as well, she thought. Now that they were back on solid ground, now that they knew Jonas was fine, everything would return to the way it was. The way it had to be.

God, she could still hear him at the dance. *We'll get married.* Did he actually think that she would stay with him just because Jonas was his son? Or because he knew now that he could give her more children? Didn't he see that a marriage for the sake of the children was a mistake for everyone involved?

She blew out a breath as Justice steered the

car down the long drive to the ranch house. Before he'd even turned off the engine, the front door flew open and a wide slice of lamplight cut into the darkness. Mrs. Carey stood on the threshold, wearing a floor-length terry cloth robe, fisted in one hand at her neck.

"Thank goodness, you're back. He's really all right?" she called out. "I've been so worried."

Maggie stepped out of the car. "He's fine, Mrs. Carey."

"Go on to bed," Justice added as he came around the front of the car. "We'll talk in the morning."

The older woman nodded and turned for the stairs, leaving the front door open with the lamplight shining like a path in the darkness.

Maggie went to the backseat, opened the door and deftly undid the straps holding Jonas in his car seat. He stirred a little, but as soon as his head was nestled onto his mother's shoulder, he went back to sleep. Having her child cuddled in close gave Maggie the strength she was going to need when she spoke to Justice. So she held on to Jonas as if he were a talisman as they headed for the house.

Once inside, Justice closed the door and silence descended on them. It had been one of the longest nights of Maggie's life—and it wasn't over yet. She couldn't wait until morning to say what had to be said. She didn't know if she'd find the will to have this conversation in the morning; by then, she might have talked herself out of it, and she couldn't allow that to happen no matter how her heart was breaking.

"Quite a night," Justice said, splintering the quiet with his deep, rumbling voice.

"Yes, it was." She turned her gaze up to his and stared into those dark blue eyes for a long moment. God, how she would miss him. *Say it now, Maggie,* she told herself firmly. *Do it and get it over with.* "Justice…"

He watched her, waiting, and she could see by his rigid stance that he wasn't expecting good news.

"I'm going to be leaving tomorrow," she said, the words bursting from her in a determined rush.

"What?" He took a step toward her, but Maggie backed up, stroking one hand up and down Jonas's spine. "Why?"

"You know why," she said sadly, feeling the sudden sting of tears. She blinked them back, desperate to at least complete this last part of their marriage with a little dignity. "Your leg's nearly healed. You don't need me, Justice, and it's time I actually moved on with my life."

"Move on?" He shook his head, ground his teeth together and said, "Now you want to move on? Now when we know I'm Jonas's father? Now that we can have the big family you always wanted?"

"It's not about that," she said with a sigh.

"I signed those divorce papers a hell of a long time ago, Maggie, but you never filed them. Why?"

She shook her head now. "You know why."

"Because you love me."

"Yes, all right?" She raised her voice and immediately regretted it when Jonas stirred against her. Hushing him, Maggie lowered her voice again and said, "I did. Still do. But when I go home, I'm finally going to file those divorce papers, Justice."

"Why now?" He stared at her, his features shadowed by the overhead light.

"Because I'm not going to stay married to you for the sake of our son," she told him, willing him to understand. "It wouldn't be right for any of us. Don't you see, Justice? I love you, but I need to be loved in return. I want to be needed. I want a man to share Jonas's life with me. I want a man who'll stand beside me—"

"Like I did tonight, you mean?"

"Yes," she said quickly, breathlessly. "Like you did tonight. But, Justice, that's not who you are normally. You don't let people in. You don't let yourself *need* anyone." She blew out a breath, bit down on her trembling lower lip and said,

"You'd rather be right than be in love. Your pride is more important to you than anything or anyone. And I can't live like that. I won't."

She turned for the stairs, her heart heavy, her soul empty. She picked up the hem of her dress, took one step and was stopped by a single word from Justice.

"Please."

Stunned to her core, Maggie slowly turned to look at him. He stood alone in the entryway, a solitary man in the shadows though he stood beneath an overhead light. There was hunger in his eyes and a taut, uncomfortable expression on his face.

She'd almost convinced herself she had imagined him speaking when he said again, louder this time, "Please stay."

Maggie swayed in place, shocked by his words, astonished that he would swallow his pride and so damn hopeful she nearly couldn't breathe. "Justice? I don't think I've ever heard you say that before."

"You haven't." Justice went to her then, desperate to make her hear him. Make her understand everything he'd learned in the past few hours. It had been coming on for days, he knew, but the time spent in that emergency room, sharing their fears, standing beside her, wanting to take on the world to help his son, had coalesced everything into a very clear vision.

Without Maggie, he had nothing.

She'd knocked the floor out from under his feet by telling him she was going to leave him again. And if he allowed it this time, he knew it would be permanent. If he clung to his pride and refused to bend, he would lose everything that had ever mattered to him.

So he threw his pride out the proverbial window and risked everything by going to her. Two long steps brought him to her side. He reached for her but stopped himself. First, he would say what she needed to hear. The words he'd denied them both the last time they were together.

"I need you, Maggie. More than my next breath I need you."

Her beautiful eyes filled with tears that crested and spilled over to roll down her cheeks unchecked. Her lower lip trembled, and he lifted one hand to soothe that lip with the pad of his thumb. His gaze moved over her, from her tumbled, tangled hair to the now-ruined elegant ball gown. She was magnificent and she was his. As she was always meant to be. This was a woman born to stand beside a man no matter what came at them in life. This was a woman to grow old with. To treasure.

To thank God for every night.

And damned if he'd lose her.

"Justice, I—"

He shook his head fiercely and spoke up, keeping his voice low so as not to disturb his son. "No, let me say this, so you'll never doubt it again. I love you more than should be humanly possible. The last time you left, you took my heart with you. When you came back,

I came alive again. I won't let you leave, Maggie. If you go, I'll go with you."

She laughed a little, tears still spilling down her cheeks, and she'd never looked more lovely to him.

"See?" he asked. "No more pride. No more anything unless you're with me."

"Oh, God…"

"Stay with me, Maggie," he said gently, tipping her chin up so that he could look into those tear-washed eyes of hers. "Please stay. Please love me again. Please let me love you and Jonas and all the other children we'll have together."

She laughed again, a small sound filled with delight and wonder, and Justice could have kicked his own ass for taking so long, for wasting so much time, before setting things right between them.

"It's getting easier to say *please*," he told her, "and I swear, tonight won't be the last time you hear it."

"I don't know what to say," she admitted, staring up at him with a smile curving her mouth and tears glistening like diamonds on her cheeks.

"Say yes," he urged, pulling her and the baby into the circle of his arms. "Say you'll stay. Say I didn't blow it this time."

She leaned her head against his chest and sighed heavily. "I love you so much."

Justice grinned and held them a little tighter. So much relief had flooded his system in the past hour that he felt almost drunk on it. He wanted to shout. He wanted to go call his brother Jeff and thank him for sending Maggie back home where she belonged.

Then she pulled back and looked up at him again. "Am I dreaming?"

He smiled at her, bent his head and placed one quick kiss on her upturned mouth. "No dream, Maggie. Just a man telling you that you are his heart. Just your husband asking you to give him another chance to prove to you that he can be the man you need. The man you deserve."

"Oh, Justice," she said with a sigh, lifting one hand to cup his cheek, "you've always been the only man for me. You've had my heart since the moment I saw you, and that will never change."

He rested his forehead against hers and gave silent thanks for coming to his senses in time.

Then Maggie shifted their son in her arms and handed him to Justice. "Why don't we take him upstairs and tuck him in? Together."

Justice cradled the tiny boy who was the second miracle in his life and dropped his free arm around Maggie's shoulders. Together, they climbed the stairs, and when they reached the landing, Maggie stopped and smiled up at him. "Once our son is settled in, I think I'm going to need a little attention from my husband."

Justice grinned at her. "I think that can be arranged."

Her head on his shoulder, they walked down the hallway of home, passing from the shadows into the light.

* * * * *

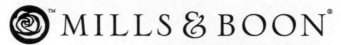